NEW VISION
PUBLICATION
P R E S E N T S

Tit 4 Tat
Payback's A Bitch
Part 2

A NOVEL BY
ALONZO L. STRANGE

ISBN: (10) 0-9826772-2-7
ISBN: (13) 978-0-9826772-2-3
Cover design: www.mariondesigns.com
Inside layout: www.mariondesigns.com
Editors: Linda Williams

Tat 4 Tat (Payback's A Bitch) a novel/Alonzo L. Strange

NEW VISION
PUBLICATION

P.O. Box 2815
Stockbridge, GA 30281
www.newvisionpublication.com

First Printing October 2010
Printed in Canada

10   9   8   7   6   5   4   3   2   1

DEDICATION

This book is dedicated to all of those that believed
and supported me through it all.

AKNOWLEDGMENTS

First and foremost, I would like to give all praises to God for keeping me focused. Without him none of this would have happened.

To my two beautiful kids, Myah Anne B. and Devin Michael B.

To my mother, the number one lady in my life. You have been there for me no matter what the situation or outcome was. I love you!

To all of the women in my life that kept me going throughout the years. Sherida H., Tania P., Helen W., and last but not least, Tracy B. Without ya'll's continuing support, I probably wouldn't have been able to fulfill my dream. Thanks for answering the phone whenever I called, for sending a brotha letters and photos making me know that I was thought about. I love you all.

To my close friends, those that have known me before all of this. I just like to say thanks.

To Karriem Barrow, my writing partner before it all. Please, get at me! Terrance "Frazier Boy" Frazier, you know I didn't forget about you. You helped me to realize that the dream could be reached. We have books to write!

To the people at New Vision Publication, thanks for giving me the opportunity to show the world, what I was capable of. This is just the beginning, I got plenty more.

This book is also dedicated to all of those that took the time out of their busy schedules to sit down, read, and enjoy what I have written.

It just wouldn't be right if I didn't thank Linda Williams, my incredible editor. I wouldn't be who I am if I didn't acknowledge you. Thanks, for believing in me and for making my dream come true.

To those of you that listened to me go on and on about the book before it was even published. People like: Aric "Bad Newz" Noel, Troy "Mr. Martinsburg WVA" Green, Yoon "Paul Park, Latif "Craig" Wortham, Daniel "Dan" Cuneo, Ben "Big Ben" Buckhanan, Roderick Long, Shane Taylors, James "Jay Dub" Watkins, and Mr. Kendall from, KC Missouri.

To all of my New York's finest, Alvon "Pop" Daniels, "Papo", Ivan Keith, Fast, Skins, Black, Melshawn, Henny, Keys and all of those that I can't possibly name on this page. Just know that, if I said more than "What's up" to you then you are being acknowledged. You know who ya'll are.

To all of my North Carolina truest, Frank "Chico" Thomas, T. Gardener, Big Woo. Wow, as I think about it, there's just too many of ya'll to name. I have come across some good people since I've been down. I just want to acknowledge those individuals that have helped or influenced me in a positive way. Thanks for keeping me grounded and focused.

When there were times that I thought that this book would never get off the ground, there was people around me constantly to tell me differently. I need to show my appreciation for telling me that this book was like that. Little do you know, those words of encouragement kept me going.

Now, to the one person that has truly impacted my life and made me respect, appreciate, and love my freedom, Agent Tateo. Thanks for helping me to realize my true potential. "You do realize that I'm just kidding right?"

A special thanks to Unique and Cheryl, at Supreme Street Books in West Palm Beach, Florida, thanks for all the love.

To the readers, I do hope that Part 2 is just as good as you thought it would be. The wait is over. *Enjoy!*

Peace,

A.L. Strange

*I only cherish the love if it's sent from up above
cause people carry a grudge, embedded in different
slugs, influenced by different drugs.*

*Now I'm staring in the eyes of the envy, a spitting
image can I turn my back, hoping that this person
don't befriend me, when a perfect world is looking
like a basement of a building, and a shinning star
reflecting lights hanging from the ceiling.*

*When the stench is coming from everyone that's
close to me, it's hard to see the light when people
cut it off on me.
So get ahead while you still have a head,
U heard that! or find yourself living the
story lines from Tit 4 Tat. . .*

*Written by: J. Ervan
(aka) Fateen Hoover*

PROLOGUE

Summer 87'

Myah was in her bedroom, laying in bed with Mr. Jingles, her favorite stuffed teddy bear, when she heard her mother's voice from down the hallway pleading for someone to stop.

"Oh my God! Pleassseee stop! Don't do this! Pleassseee!!! Don't do this!" Each time she heard, "Don't do this!" A loud smack would follow with a male's voice saying "Shut-up! Shut-tha-fuck-up!" Smack! "Ughhh! Oh my Go…" Smack! "So you thought you could play me huh?" The voice asked between clenched teeth in a poor attempt of trying to be quiet.

With all of the noise that her mother was making, Myah decided to be curious and see what was going on.

As she grabbed Mr. Jungles and got from under the covers, she quietly made her way down the hallway. She noticed that her mother's bedroom door was slightly opened. Usually when her mother and her boyfriend were in there, the door would be completely shut, but since it wasn't, Myah wanted to see why her mother was always moaning or screaming whenever her boyfriend was over.

She slowly walked up to the door, peeped through the crack, and what Myah saw made her eyes grow big and her mouth turn dry. Her mother was crying with blood covering her face, while a man, that Myah never seen before, was on top of her naked body holding her down trying to force himself inside of her.

She saw her mother trying to fight the stranger off, but he continued to beat her repeatedly in the face until her mother's body went limp. The tears started to flow from Myah's eyes as she stood frozen in place watching the strange man beat on her mother's lifeless body.

When he turned towards the door and looked at her as if he knew she was there watching, she saw the long scar that ran down the side of his face which scared her even more. That's when Myah slowly backed away from the door, ran back to her room, into her closet, and hid amongst the things strewed about the bottom, trying her best to hide from the monster that was in her mother's bedroom.

She didn't dare make a sound, hoping that whoever it was would leave without finding her. Even the sound of the front door closing still wasn't enough to bring Myah out of her safe place.

Only when it was completely quiet was when she even thought about coming out. Just as she was about to see if the coast was clear, she heard foot steps coming down the hallway towards her bedroom.

Trying not to move, Myah lost her balance and bumped into a shoe box which caused it to fall and make a loud noise. The voice she heard this time was very much different from the voice she had heard in her mother's bedroom earlier.

"This is the police! Come out with your hands in the air now!" Not wanting the bad man to find her, Myah stayed quiet. When whomever it was that was talking opened the closet door, Myah held Mr. Jingles tightly and closed her eyes shut hoping that for once, she was invisible....

ONE

"If I didn't know any better, I'd swear you two were fucking especially by the way you're standing up for her and all." Was the last thing Myah kept hearing over and over again in her head as she drove the Southern State Parkway, heading towards the Bronx to see Irk.

The hatred in her heart that she was feeling was all because of Keisha. Just the way she acted earlier made Myah suspicious, especially more now after she thought about the little post-it note she found on her locker.

After putting two and two together, Myah began to see that Keisha was the one behind the notes, pictures, and the extortion attempt. Even though she couldn't prove it, in her heart, she was 100% sure that Keisha was behind it.

As she continued to drive over the Throgs Neck Bridge and onto Gun Hill Road, her mind was racing a mile-a-minute with all she had going on. Between the things her and Nikki had done, Keisha's extortion plot, Irk and Henry, Myah was starting to show clear signs of stress.

When she finally reached her destination, she had calmed down some. The long drive helped a little to relieve some of the tension she was feeling, but she knew that once she was with Irk, he would help her to forget about all that was bothering her. So she sat in her car for an extra couple of minutes, just to clear her thoughts of what happened at school.

Once she felt in control, she got out and proceeded to walk into her apartment building knowing that relief was just an orgasm away.

The next day at school, Myah went about her morning, as usual. She met up with Nikki and a couple of other girls that she hung out with. Last night at her apartment, she and Irk stayed in bed until eleven at night, and did everything imaginable that they could sexually think of to each other. Myah was so spent, that when she finally made it back to her aunt and uncle's house at one in the morning, she collapsed onto her canopy bed and slept until just about two hours ago. She only had time to wash her face and change her clothes.

Her pussy was sore from the pounding that Irk gave her. The stamina that he had wasn't normal, she thought to herself. Myah decided to wear a skirt with no panties in order to let her pussy breathe. She didn't want to worry about it rubbing against any fabric. She sprayed some feminine spray down there since she didn't get a chance to bathe, but she wasn't too worried about it smelling. *My pussy smells good, even when it's beat tha fuck up!* She thought to herself as she walked down the hallway towards her locker.

The smile on her face caused the other girls to ask questions. "Hey, Myah, you look as if you just got some good dick. What's the story?" Amy asked once they stopped near Julie's locker.

Amy was a petite young black girl, who grew up around money. She didn't hang around too many blacks, so her vocabulary was sort of whitish. She was five-four, and weighed about one-hundred and twenty-five pounds. Her biggest asset were her tits. For a small frame, her tits looked huge. Amy was cute, but her attitude deterred a lot of people from approaching her. Guys were intimidated, while girls were jealous. That's probably why Myah became good friends with her.

"Damn, girlfriend! Is it that obvious?" Myah replied, smiling like she was guilty as charged.

"Oooo, you bitch! Give us the details!" Amy shouted.

Before Myah could say another word, she saw Keisha walking towards them, smiling. She was surrounded by Tanya, Mimi, Yolanda and Stacy, her little entourage. Myah was prepared for a fight, if need be, but she knew she wasn't dressed for one. She stood with her back to the lockers, waiting for whatever to go down.

Keisha and her small group never broke stride. In fact, she greeted Myah, Amy, Julie and Nikki with a smirk as she walked past them to her homeroom class. Tanya, Mimi and Yolanda waved and followed along as if Keisha was their fearless leader.

Myah's body was tense, but she was relieved that it didn't go down right at that moment. She was really trying to keep her promise to her aunt about not fighting. The many times that she did have fights were because of how someone disrespected her or someone was jealous of her. Most of the fights could have been avoided, but Myah had something to prove, and everyone knew that she wasn't just a pretty face. She could handle herself if the need arose. But after countless ISS (In-School Suspen-sions), and being sent home, Myah's aunt was fed up with it and made Myah promise to do better, or she would be sent to a different school. Myah knew her aunt's threats weren't to be taken lightly. Her aunt was a pillar in the school system, and everyone from the schools' superintendent to the janitor respected her. If she wanted it done, she got it done.

Myah relaxed a little once she saw Keisha and her little crew turn the corner. Even though she wanted to confront her about the pictures and the notes that she had been sending her and Nikki, she knew that this wasn't the time nor the place to do it.

Amy, who saw how she reacted, was the first to ask a question. "Hey, girl, is everything alright?"

Myah looked at her, straightened out her skirt and said, "Yeah, I'm cool. Why?"

"I don't know. It just looked like you were nervous about something. I thought you and Keisha were friends." Amy waited for an answer.

Nikki knew exactly what Myah was thinking before Myah could answer Amy's question. She said, "Hey, Myah, we have to get going before they ring the bell for homeroom. I have to holler at you before we go."

Myah nodded her head to indicate okay. As she opened her locker to get her books, Amy looked around and saw Julie standing off to the side. "Yeah, I better get going too. Julie, you ready?" Amy asked while preparing to turn around to go back the way they had come.

Julie was a medium sized white girl who was Amy's right hand girl. Wherever Amy went, Julie was sure to follow. Every good person needs a sidekick.

"Yeah, I'm ready!" Julie shouted as she gathered her books in her arms.

Julie and Amy gave Myah and Nikki good-bye hugs and left them standing at the lockers. Once they were out of earshot, Myah grunted through clenched teeth. She knew that she couldn't take it out on Nikki, so she did the next best thing and hit the lockers, which gave her a little relief.

"What's the matter with you?" Nikki screamed,

trying to figure out why Myah was acting like she was. "That bitch is *dead!* Do you hear me? *Dead!* As God is my witness, that bitch is gonna get what she deserves!"

The look in Myah's eyes as she said those words made Nikki cringe inside. She knew that Myah was serious about what she was saying, even though she never saw Myah this mad before. Somehow, she knew that Myah meant ever word.

Trish and her crew of three other girls arrived at Half Hollow Hills East High School just as the lunch period was starting. They drove from Brooklyn's Boys and Girls High School in Tamika's '99 hunter green Jeep Cherokee Limited. They all piled in that morning and drove to Long Island with the anticipation of beating down some girl that Trish had beef with.

"Just make sure that no one brings blood back into my Jeep!" Tamika stated as she parked the SUV down the road from the school.

"Ah, bitch! No one's gonna mess up your shit. Just make sure you do something this time. Don't think that we didn't see how your ass punked out on that last fight we had with those bitches from Queens," Trish said, laughing.

The other girls, Danella and Marketa, who were in the back seat, laughed out loud as they remembered that fight.

"Yeah, Tamika, your ass ran as soon as that fat bitch pulled out her razor. I looked around and thought you were gone until I seen you behind that building," Danella added as she opened the door to step out.

"Yo ass was ghost!" Marketa said to emphasize the point.

"That bitch was big as hell! Shit, no one saw the way that she jumped up. It was like she was a man in drag!" Tamika replied, trying to justify her actions.

After locking the Jeep, they proceeded to walk towards the back of the school, which was huge compared to their rundown school in Brooklyn.

"Damn! You see how big this school is, Trish?" Marketa asked as they walked through what looked to be the faculty parking lot.

"Yeah, it looks like a college campus."

All of the cars they passed were either brand new or only a couple of years old. Then, Danella noticed that the cars had student parking tickets on them. "What tha fuck! These are the students' cars! Damn!"

"The parents let their kids drive Mercedes Benz's, Audi's, BMW's, and other high priced cars to school? I can imagine what their houses look like if they let their kids drive these," Tamika said.

"Bitch, look what you're driving!" Trish stated loudly.

"Yeah, but you know that it's my sister's shit. Her man bought that for her. You know what he do."

"Then why tha fuck are you driving it?" Trish asked.

"'Cause she's at his crib and wanted me to get lost," Tamika replied. So, I took her shit since I knew she'd be there for a minute."

"What happens if she's ready to go and you're no where to be found? She's gonna beat that ass! You know how Tincy gets down," Marketa stated.

"She's not gonna do shit, unless she wants me to rat her ass out to my dad. She knows better than to act tha fuck up. Besides, we'll be back before three, right?" Tamika asked as they rounded the back of the building.

Trish was the first to notice three girls smoking cigarettes near the benches that were locked in front of what appeared to be a student-made handball court.

"Ayo!" Trish said quietly, trying to get the other girls' attention, but since they were talking amongst themselves, they didn't hear her. "Will y'all shut the fuck up and listen!" she shouted just loud enough for them to hear. "I'ma go and ask these girls if they know where this bitch, Keisha is. Y'all stay here. Tamika, give me one of your Newports."

Tamika reached into the front of her jeans and pulled out her box of Newports and handed them to Trish. Once she did, Trish started to walk towards the three girls, leaving Tamika, Danella and Marketa standing at the top of the hill.

As Trish approached the three girls who were sitting around the bench, she did a quick survey of the area to make sure there was no one else around, just in case one of them was in fact, Keisha. Trish had the Newport in one hand, while in her mouth was a single edge razor that she loved to use. She was so good at concealing it in her mouth that no one ever knew that she had it unless she told them. She didn't slur her words or even cut herself while she held it.

When she was close enough to them, she greeted them with, "Hey, can I get a light from someone?" She knew that they would hesitate at first, since she didn't go to their school, but she also knew that smokers shared a certain bond. You never deny a smoker a light.

The girl closest to Trish pulled out her lighter and placed it in front of the cigarette that Trish held up. Once it was lit, Trish took a deep pull and let out a cloud of smoke. "Whew! I've been dying for a smoke all day," she said as she looked from one girl to the next, trying to get a read on them.

Tamika, Marketa and Danella were watching everything from the top of the hill, waiting for the signal to come down. "What tha fuck is taking so long?" Marketa asked as she squinted her eyes to get a better look.

"Don't worry, Trish can handle herself pretty well. If there's a problem, she'll call us," Danella stated in a calm voice. She knew Trish better than the other two.

"I just want to get this shit over with and be out," Tamika added. She looked at her watch and noticed that it was approaching noon. She knew that if she wasn't back by at least three, her sister was going to beat her ass.

When Trish asked her if she could drive out to Long Island, she should have said no, but she didn't want Trish to think bad about her, so she agreed and took her sister's truck. Tamika told her that she was just going to pick up a friend real quick, but that was two hours ago, and Trish knew that her sister would be wanting her shit real soon.

While all of that was going on behind the school, Keisha and her crew were just finishing lunch. Keisha needed a cigarette badly, especially after eating two slices of pizza with extra cheese, and a sixteen-ounce diet Pepsi. Since no one she hung out with smoked, she decided to meet them later, and headed around to the back of the school where all of the smokers went to puff. As she made her way towards the door that would lead her out back, she saw Bree'Ann coming towards her, trying to get her attention.

"Hey, Keisha! Some girls are out back looking for you. I told them I would get you since I know they aren't from here."

"Did they tell you their names?" Keisha asked, trying to figure out who they could be. She wasn't expecting anyone, so it was strange.

"They look like they are from Wyandanch, so I thought you would know them," Bree'Ann added when she saw the puzzled look on Keisha's face. "A'ight. Thanks, Bree'Ann. Good looking out," Keisha said as she continued out the door towards the handball court where all the burn-outs smoked.

Trish had gotten one of the girls to go get Keisha after she found out that none of them were her. She called her crew down once she saw that it was starting to get crowded where she was standing. She didn't want them looking suspicious.

While a girl named Bree'Ann went to get their victim, Trish made small talk with the other two that stayed. "What grade y'all in?" she asked them.

The one with the long brown hair said, "I'm in the tenth."

The other girl with the short black hair and brown eyes said, "Me too."

Tamika, Marketa and Danella were sitting on the bench listening to them talk, just smiling. The two girls felt uncomfortable, since they knew that they were definitely out of place amongst Trish and her crew. As soon as they saw Keisha coming down the walkway, they said their goodbyes, and headed back inside to get ready for their next class.

Keisha still didn't recognize any of the girls that were sitting on the bench. She thought that maybe Vida had sent them, but she knew how to call her cell phone if she needed her. It didn't matter. Since she was out there, she was going to find out and smoke her cigarette as she did so. She pulled out her Capri cigarettes and lit one up as she got closer to the bench. Once she was there, she realized that she didn't know any of them. Keisha became physically nervous as she tried to figure out what they wanted with her.

"Are you Keisha Green?" Trish asked in a friendly tone of voice.

Once Keisha confirmed that she was, Trish spit the razor into her right hand and jumped up. Tamika, Marketa and Danella surrounded Keisha as Trish said, "Well, I guess this is your unlucky day!" and brought the razor straight across Keisha's face. Trish knew how to hold it to where it wouldn't do severe damage, but it would get the point across in a painful way.

The first slice stunned Keisha, who didn't realize that her face had just been cut. The razor was so sharp that it went straight across in a clean motion, leaving a shallow slice from one side of her face to the other. Keisha tried to back up, but Tamika and the rest of the girls were right there to stop her.

"A mutual friend sends their love... *bitch!*" Trish said jokingly as she once again came across Keisha's face.

Keisha held her hand up in defense just in time, so instead of going across her face, it sliced open her hand. She screamed out loud, hoping that someone would stop them, but Trish was on top of her as Keisha felt blood covering her eyes and running down her face. She tried to fight, but all she could do was cover up and hope that her attacker would stop.

When others saw what was going on, they rushed over to watch the fight. No one dared jump in for fear that it would happen to them, but what they witnessed was not a pretty sight at all. Keisha was covered in blood as she lay in a fetal position. The four girls that did this had run up the hill before the crowd made their way over.

"Someone go get the nurse!" a young girl shouted. Another girl came over to comfort Keisha, but once she saw the cuts on her face and hands, she too stayed back until help arrived.

TWO

A lot had happened since the last time that Detective Williamson had seen Myah. As he was sitting in his recliner at home, watching The Late Show, he was thinking back on the meeting he had with her. What baffled him the most was the fact that after telling her about Anderson's parole hearing, she acted as if she knew about it beforehand. She seemed too calm when he told her his theory of who he thought killed her mother. There were many questions that haunted his thoughts about that meeting, so he was now more determined to find out the answers.

When he had some free time from the cases he was working on, he did some investigating into Myah Johnson's background. He knew what she'd been through, but who were her friends, and what did she do besides go to school? Where did she hang out, and why did she need to know things about a case that was years old?

He knew that something wasn't right with her, so he did some snooping, and what he found out shocked him. Myah had been writing Anderson for the past two years. Her phone records showed that she'd been receiving calls from a known drug dealer that has been on the city's hot list for quite some time. What was Myah up to and why was she involving herself with criminals such as Dirk Wright, a.k.a. Irk? No matter what, Detective Williamson knew that Myah was definitely not as innocent as he thought she was. "What are you up to, Myah?" he asked himself as he flicked the television off and got up from his chair to head to bed. Whenever he had trouble thinking, Detective Williamson would come to his TV room to think.

His wife, Christina, was upset with him because he was spending too much time with job-related issues than with his own family. She had warned him time and time again that she would leave him if he didn't pay more attention to what was going on at home. Somehow, he didn't take her seriously, and now she and their two boys were staying at her mother's in Brooklyn until he decided what truly mattered most.

Williamson had trouble separating the two; his life at home and his life as a cop. His life as an officer was all he thought about when he first started twelve years ago. But after he became a detective, he worked even harder to stay ahead and prove to those that gave him the opportunity to show what he could do, that they were right in believing in him. He thought his wife understood this, but as time passed, she started to become more and more impatient with him and his job than she did before.

With the separation of he and his wife going into its third week, he found himself thinking about the possibility of divorce. He knew that he would just be holding his wife back from doing what she really wanted to do. She would just resent their marriage and become another bitter person because of it, so the thought of divorce was starting to seem more and more the better option. This reasoning was probably why he focused more of his time into his work.

He laid across his king-size bed that he and his wife had shared for the last eleven years. He fell asleep on his side of the bed, since his body had been programmed to it for so long, even though he was physically aware that his wife was not coming back any time soon. He felt guilty for having dreams of Myah. This made him even more determined than before to figure out the true relationship between her and Anderson.

The next day, Williamson walked into his precinct and was immediately told to report to the captain's office, which was located one floor above his office.

"Captain, what's up?" Williamson greeted once he was admitted into his office by the captain's personal secretary. Alaina Kindrell was in her early forties, with shoulder-length reddish brown curly hair. Her hair had been dyed to cover the early stages of graying. She obviously kept herself in shape by the figure that she had. Her body was that of a twenty-year old. Nice tits, a small waist, and a voluptuous ass rounded out the dimensions of her figure perfectly. With her caramel complexion, she was definitely pleasing to look at. Detective Williams and a few others who had the opportunity to work around her on a regular basis had been caught by the captain more than once, ogling his secretary.

"Detective, there's been a homicide over in the Soundview Projects. I want you to personally conduct the investigation on this one," Captain Grey informed him as he slid the detective a piece of paper.

"What's this?" Williamson asked as he took it from off the desk.

"That's the name of the therapist that helped me to get my life back after the divorce of me and my wife."

"I don't understand," Williamson said.

It was common knowledge what was going on with

Williamson's marriage, since the precinct was a close knit family.

"I've noticed how you've been moving around here lately, and I just figured that it would be of some help."

"I appreciate it, but no thanks," he said, then slid the paper back on the desk.

The captain gathered some papers without looking back up, and said, "Well, why are you still here? Get out of here and take care of your business."

Williamson stood up, smiled, and walked out of the door, past Alaina, giving her a smile as he walked towards the stairway to go down to his office.

Byron Pitts, a.k.a. Young Bizarini, was on his way to his girl's crib out in Queens in his '96 bowling ball green Acura Legend. He was stuck in traffic on the BQE (Brooklyn/Queens Expressway) when he received a call on his cell phone. He had it on vibrate since his system was on full blast, pumping that new single by Joe and Big Pun, "I'm Not a Playa, I just Crush A Lot". He felt it against his waist and quickly took it out to see who it was. It was his man, Big Cee from his 'hood. "Ayo, son, what's good?" Bizarini asked as he turned down the volume on his system.

Big Cee was back around the way, holding down the blocks and making that paper that Bizarini was missing out on since he had business to take care of. At least that's what he told Big Cee when he jumped in his car to get ghost.

"The block is swarming with five-O, son!" Big Cee said excitedly as he looked nervously out of the window of the bodega on the corner.

Young Bizarini just turned down a residential block and found a place to park his whip as he continued to listen to his boy describe the scene.

"Sadell just got smoked about an hour ago. Son, his body is still laying in the building's doorway! Somebody put two hot ones in his dome, kid! That shit's crazy! Word's bond, son!"

Bizarini's body went numb hearing all of this news from his boy. The first question that came to his mind was, "Do they know who did it?"

"Nah, but I think someone saw the shooter. There's some DT's questioning some people right now," Cee answered.

Bizarini started to sweat profusely. He was quiet for a few minutes, which caused his boy, Cee to ask, "Ayo, Biz, you still there, son?"

"Yeah, yeah, yeah, I'm still here. Yo, Cee, find out who five-O's talking to, a'ight?"

"You got that. Why? What's the dilly-O?" Cee asked, suspicious of his boy's reaction to the news of one of his own being knocked off. Something just wasn't right, but Cee wasn't going to ask questions. He's been in the game long enough, and saw too much to start asking about a murder, no matter who it was.

"Ayo, Big Cee, just find out for me, a'ight? I gotta go. I'll hit you back later. One!" Bizarini flipped his phone closed and stared out of his tinted window at his girl's crib. His mind was racing, trying to figure out if anyone had seen him, or if he saw anyone before or after he popped Sadell in the head inside the doorway of his own apartment building.

What made him so good was the fact that he was very discrete about his business. He never had feelings for any of his victims before, but since this was one of his own peeps, someone that he broke bread with on many occasions, it was a little harder for him to swallow. Even though the pill was hard to swallow when Irk gave him the order, it had to be done, so he tried to make it as quick and painless as possible. He knew the heat would be around asking questions, but he never figured that someone would see him and point him out as the shooter. "Leave no witnesses" was his motto, and Bizarini planned on living by that motto.

Detective Williamson was at the crime scene within half an hour of getting the assignment from the captain. Dressed in his white Brooks Brother's dress shirt and a pair of black slacks that were tailor-made for him, he was escorted over to the victim's body that was still laying in the building's doorway and covered by a white sheet. "Has the coroner arrived yet?" he quickly asked as he put on a pair of white latex gloves.

"She's on her way, Detective," the Young officer who was escorting him answered before lifting up the yellow police tape for Williamson to go under.

"Who was the first on the scene? And were there any witnesses that you know of?"

"Well, sir, Officer Keaton and Officer Palmer are right over there." He pointed with his right hand towards a group of officers talking amongst themselves. Detective Williamson looked in the direction that the officer pointed and nodded his head. "As far as the witnesses go, you know how the projects are, sir. They don't want to be the next, so no one's talking."

"Get on your radio and call the officers that were here first on the scene and tell them to come over here. I want to know what they saw first," the detective said while he examined the body and surrounding area. Within two minutes, he was joined by the two officers that were the first to arrive.

Officer Keaton, an eight-year vet with the precinct was the first to volunteer his services. "Hey, Detective, how can I help you?"

Williamson looked at him and asked, "When you first arrived, did you secure the crime scene?"

The seasoned officer smirked and said, "Sure did, Detective."

Williamson looked him in the eyes and said, "Well, where are the shell casings for the bullets?"

"Officer Keaton's expression turned from sarcastic to confusion within a matter of seconds. "I... I... I don't know, Detective. We just called the murder in."

Williamson knew that no one secured the scene right away, because of the heavy traffic that was evident around the body and immediate area. "Well, Officer..." Williamson looked at his nameplate on his shirt, and then continued in a calm voice, "...Keaton, is it?"

"Yes, sir. Officer Joseph Keaton."

"Okay, Officer Joseph Keaton. I want you to move anyone that has nothing to do with this case back so that no one can tamper with anything that might be useful to us. Then, I want the forensics team here ASAP. Can you handle that, Officer Joseph Keaton?" Detective Williamson talked in an even tone, as if Keaton was a young child, which wasn't lost on the officer's part.

"Right away, Detective. Is that it?" he asked before he turn to go back to his patrol car.

"Yes, that will be all!" Williamson barked.

Officer Keaton turned around and said under his breath once he knew that the detective couldn't hear him,

"Asshole!"

Williamson knew that he wasn't liked very much, but he also knew that he was good at his job, and that was all that mattered to him.

While all of this was going on across town, Irk was sitting on a bench in front of his projects, smoking on a blunt and sipping on a Heineken. He was waiting for Big Zo to come back from the bodega that was just a minute up the block. He went to get a pack of squares (cigarettes) and a box of Philly Blunts. Just as Irk was about to clip the rest of the blunt, Big Zo came strolling through with a smirk on his face and a fresh Philly sliced open. "Hey, son! What took you so long?" Irk asked once he was able to keep the blunt lit so his boy could hit it.

"Yo, Irk, I heard that your boy, Sadell, just got hit up and the word is that he's now taking a permanent rest from the streets!" Big Zo said laughing.

Irk wasn't surprised. In fact, he was happy to hear that his peoples took care of their business. "Sometimes the streets take care of their own, and in the process, they also implement their own justice."

"So in other words, they hold court for those accused in the streets, huh?" Zo asked, trying to rationalize exactly what Irk was talking about.

They both started laughing, because they both knew that Irk was the judge, jury and executioner all in one. Whatever he said was law. Whatever he needed to be done was done, and whoever had to be dealt with, was dealt with. It was Sadell's turn to feel Irk's wrath since he didn't respect the game.

Irk had met Young Bizarini a couple of years ago at a club out in Queens. Just as he was about to leave with his entourage, a fight broke out, which led to guns being drawn. As Irk's people scrambled to protect him, Irk witnessed a young kid creeping in the background shoot up his victim and dip out, all without being seen. The silencer on his gun was so quiet that not even the victim's own people knew that he had been hit. The fight was just staged to distract the crowd in order for this young killer to do his work. From that day on, Irk respected the young one's hustle.

Later, Irk found out that the shooter was a young cat named Byron that would do just about any hit you wanted, for the right price. He made it his business to meet this young kid, which became a reality about a year later. While being introduced to an old hustler out in Queens, it just so happened that the kid that Irk had seen at the club a year ago was now staring at him. They were introduced to one another, and once Irk was alone with him, he told the young kid how he saw his work firsthand. Irk was impressed with how the Young kid handled himself, and before he knew it, he gave the young kid a job working for him as his personal clean-up man. Irk also gave him the name "Young Bizarini" because of how he disappeared after doing a hit, just like Houdini. And since his name was "Byron", Irk put the two names together and called him "Bizarini" so he could stop calling him "young kid".

Ever since then, their relationship has been a good one. Whenever Irk called upon the young hit man, he never disappointed, and when there were moments of nothing, Irk put him on the blocks to make money for himself.

When Irk called yesterday and told his young hit man his intended victim's name, he knew the job would get done nice and discretely. So, upon hearing the news from his most trusted lieutenant, Big Zo, Irk knew that Young Bizarini had handled his business.

THREE

Myah heard of Keisha's attack after her fourth period class with Mr. McGrath. She was going towards the cafeteria when she saw everyone gathering around the window, trying to catch a glimpse of something. As she continued to walk into the lunchroom, she noticed that her crew of girls, Keisha, Nikki, Tanya and Mimi, were nowhere in sight. She saw Iliana, an exotic Romanian with jet black hair, high cheekbones and a thin but athletic build, walking towards her with a look of shock on her face. "Iliana, what's wrong?" Myah asked excitedly, trying to figure out why everyone was acting so strangely.

"You haven't heard?" Iliana replied in an upset tone of voice. "Keisha just got jumped by four girls! They cut her face up real bad! They're taking her to the hospital right now!"

"Have you seen Nikki, Tanya or Mimi?" Myah frantically asked, hoping to get some more information on Keisha's condition.

Iliana shook her head "no" then continued out of the lunchroom and disappeared down the hall.

Just as Myah was about to go back inside, she heard someone call out her name. "Myah! Myyyyahhh!" Myah whipped her head around so fast that her hair almost smacked her in the face once she stopped. Nikki was weaving her way through the throng of students that were being nosy. "Myah, did you hear what happened to Keisha?" Nikki asked as she tried to catch her breath.

"Yeah! What tha fuck happened?"

"I don't know, but I thought it was you when I heard about the fight. Once they told me that her face was sliced up and that four girls jumped her, I knew it wasn't you," Nikki answered excitedly, giving Myah a late hug.

"Gee, thanks! Do they know who did it?"

"Not that I know of, but I only heard bits and pieces of the story. I had to leave to find you." Nikki smiled, knowing that it wasn't Myah that was involved, but was somewhat suspicious about the whole situation, since Myah did threaten to get even with Keisha earlier.

Myah and Nikki both felt bad about what went down with Keisha. Myah knew that everyone would think that she had something to do with what happened, since she and Keisha had some words. Tanya and Mimi acted funny when Myah asked them about the incident. It was as if they were afraid to talk to her. She just shrugged it off, thinking it was because they were upset. But in fact, it was because they too thought that Myah had something to do with what happened to their friend.

When Myah got back to her house, she went straight to her room, not wanting to be bothered. She collapsed on her bed and fell asleep. It was 5:22 in the evening when she finally woke up. She heard her cell phone ringing from inside her bag. After grabbing it, she read the readout and saw that it was Irk calling. "Hello!" she answered in a sleepy voice.

"Hey, Princess! What's up?"

Myah was happy to hear his voice, and as she sat up

in her bed to talk, she looked over towards her clock on the nightstand and realized that she'd been asleep for over two hours. "Hi, baby! Where you at?"

"I'm in tha 'hood. I just called to see how you were doing." Irk wanted to find out if Trish had taken care of her business.

Myah had a smile on her face. Her body felt tired, but she knew that she wanted to get with him so that he could hold her and put that big dick of his inside of her. "Well, I could use a little sumptin' sumptin', if you know what I mean!" she said in her most seductive voice. Her right hand went down to her pussy, and she rubbed her clit through her jeans, anticipating his response.

"Yeah, you ain't trying to do nothing," Irk playfully said as he looked out of his car window towards a group of girls that were walking towards him. He was sitting in the parking lot of Kentucky Fried Chicken, waiting for Big Zo to come out with their food. He thought about how he was going to find out what he wanted without letting Myah know what he did. "Did you have any more problems with that girl, Keisha today?"

Myah almost forgot about what happened to Keisha until Irk asked that question. "No, but some girls came to the school and sliced up her face real bad. She's in the hospital right now. As a matter of fact, I have to find out how she's doing. I feel real bad about what happened, even though we had beef."

Irk smiled because he knew that Trish had kept her word, and now he would have to keep his and bless her tonight like he promised. "Oh yeah? Do they know who did it?" he asked as an afterthought.

"No, but they think it was some girls from Wyandanch that she hung out with."

"Damn! What ever did she do to them? It must'a

been bad. Payback's a bitch!" Irk said with a smile.

"Yeah, I guess so," Myah replied as she continued to play with her pussy on the bed. Just as she was about to tell him that she needed to see him tonight, her phone beeped, indicating that someone was on the other line. "Hey, baby, hold on for one minute." She clicked over to answer the call. "Hello!"

"Hey, Myah, what's up?" Nikki asked in a sullen voice.

"Hey, Nik. Let me call you back in five minutes. I'm on the phone with Irk."

"Alright. Bye-e-e!" Nikki hung up and thought to herself that she had to get Myah to see that Irk was no good for her.

Myah clicked back over and heard Irk talking to someone. "Did they have those spicy BBQ chicken fingers?"

Big Zo jumped in the car and pulled out Irk's bag to hand to him. "Hell yeah! You know I had to get some of those!" he said excitedly.

"That's what's up!" Irk replied as he put the phone back to his ear. "Hello! Hello!"

"Yeah, baby, I'm here. Did you get me something to eat too?" Myah asked jokingly.

"Nah, Princess, but I got something for you tomorrow, a'ight?"

"What do you mean, 'tomorrow'? I can't see you tonight?" she quickly asked.

"I have something I have to take care of tonight, but I will be over at your apartment tomorrow. Are you coming through after school?"

Myah was pissed, but she played it off. "Yeah, I'll come through tomorrow. What time?"

"Around eight. I got something for you, Princess."

Irk knew that she was pissed, so he had to make up for it.
"What is it?" she asked, wanting badly to know.

"I'll show you tomorrow," Irk replied as he pulled out of the parking lot and into the Bronx traffic. "Let me get going. I have some stops to make right now, but I'll get at'cha later, a'ight?"

"Yeah. I'll holla at'cha. Bye!" Myah said, and hung up the phone, upset and horny.

Once the phone clicked off, Irk called Trish. It rang three times before she finally picked up.

"Yeah, what's up?"

Irk wasn't really feeling her right now, but a promise was a promise and he had to keep his word. "Trish, be in front of your crib at eight. If you're not there, I'm out."

"That's what's up!" Trish said, hardly trying to contain her excitement.

"And Trish have someone for my man, Big Zo. He's coming with me, or can you handle both of us?" Irk asked, looking over at his man, smiling, since he knew Big Zo was listening.

"I could, but I want some quality time with you, so I'll get my girl, Marketa to come."

"A'ight! Eight sharp, not a minute later!" Irk reiterated before hanging up the phone.

Since Myah was disappointed that she wouldn't be able to be with Irk, she got out of her bed, took off her clothes and proceeded to finger herself to an orgasm. After satisfying herself, she took a quick shower and got dressed and called Nikki. The time on her clock read 7:31 p.m. as she waited for Nikki to answer her phone. Once she did, Myah told her that she'd be at her house within a half-hour. Then she hung up and went downstairs to fix herself something to eat. After putting together a quick sandwich that she devoured within minutes, she went to her aunt's room to tell her that she was going over to Nikki's house for a couple of hours.

"Hey, baby. I'm sorry to hear what happened to your friend, Keisha," her aunt said as she put down some papers that she was grading at her desk.

Myah's uncle was laying in bed in his pajamas, reading the newspaper when Myah came in, but once he heard his wife say that, he looked up and placed the paper to the side. "Myah, were you involved in that incident at all?" her uncle asked in a worried voice.

"No, Uncle John. I didn't know anything about it until I went to the cafeteria after my fourth period class."

"Well, I want you to stay home for a couple of days until I find out what's going on, okay?" her aunt jumped in.

"Aunt Mary, I have to take my biology test Friday! I can't miss that!"

"I'll talk to Mr. Stilly. I'm sure he'll understand and let you take it next week."

Somehow, Myah was relieved to be taking a couple of days off. Her grades were good enough. Plus, with prom coming up soon, it'll give her some time to plan something. At first she wasn't going to go, but that was before she met Irk.

"Yeah, I agree with Mary. A couple of days out of school wouldn't hurt," her uncle stated as he picked up the section of the paper that he was reading earlier. "Besides, I'm sure you have some things you want to catch up on. How's the car running?"

"Ah, it's good. I love it. I'm taking it to Car-Tunes this weekend to get another stereo put in!" Myah said excitedly.

"Car-Tunes! What's wrong with the radio that came with the car? I paid for the best system they had," John retorted, sounding disappointed that he still didn't get it right.

"The system—I mean—the radio that they put in was good, but you know... it just wasn't loud enough," Myah tried to explain, but knew that her aunt and uncle just wouldn't understand.

"Wasn't loud enough! I swear! You kids today! That's why every one of y'all are walking around here now, half deaf!" her aunt added as she turned back around towards her desk.

Myah looked at her watch and remembered that she had to get going. "I gotta go! I'll see you in a couple of hours. Bye-e-e!"

"Drive safely!" her aunt yelled as Myah went down to the stairs towards her room.

As Myah grabbed her Coach bag that contained her car keys and cell phone, she looked over on her nightstand and noticed the letter that Henry had written. She promised herself that she would write him a letter tomorrow, but right now, she had to get going. She closed the door to her room after cutting the lights off, and went down the stairs to get in her car that was parked in the driveway.

After staying over at Nikki's for about three hours, Myah returned home and found her aunt and uncle were already in bed, asleep. She quietly went up the stairs to her room, took off her clothes and hopped into bed. Even though it was late, she just wasn't tired. She picked up the letter that Henry wrote and read it again. When she finished, she got up, went over to her desk and sat down to write a letter to the man that had hurt her the most:

Dear Hendrick;

I know it's been a minute since I last wrote you. I'm sorry it took me this long to write back. After my party, which was tha bomb, *I just got sidetracked with school and getting ready to graduate. I doubt that I'll be going to the prom, since you aren't out here to take me...*

Myah smiled at the comment she wrote about the prom, knowing that she could care less about him going with her. She was good at playing the game with him, but she knew that there was going to come a time when she would have to act for real. Right now, it was easy to pretend, but once Henry is out of prison, that's when the real acting will commence. She continued with the rest of the letter, explaining along the way about things that were important for him to know, answering all of the questions he had asked in his letter, and asking some of her own as well.

After all was written, she had a five page letter ready to be mailed out in the morning to the Elmira State Penitentiary. She planned on going to the post office in Wyandanch where she mailed all of her letters to him. This was so that he couldn't find out the exact address of her aunt and uncle's house. She'd been doing this for the past two years, ever since Nikki had gotten her car and was able to drive alone during the day.

Myah made sure that Henry knew that she planned on coming to visit him very soon, since she was going to a college that was about three hours way from him. Her plans of gaining his trust were working like she wanted, and now was the real test. If she could fool him into believing that she truly wanted to be with him, then all of the things she did would have been worth it.

That night, Myah went to sleep, dreaming of her and Irk together sexually at her apartment. Then, just as she was getting into it, visions of Henry jumped into her dream, causing her to wonder if it meant something. The rest of the night, she slept quietly, forgetting about everything, and thinking of nothing.

FOUR

On Saturday, Keisha was released from the hospital after undergoing countless surgeries to repair her face and hands. She had sustained severe muscle, nerve and tendon damage from the deep slashing of the razor that Trish had used. Her face and hands were wrapped in gauze to protect the cuts from infection. Her mother came to bring her home, and while in the car, Keisha never said a word. She didn't want to see what she looked like, because she knew that she wouldn't be able to handle the sight if she did.

As they drove on the Southern State Parkway, heading back to Wheatly Heights, Keisha looked out of the window and thought about everything that led up to her being like she was now. *The pictures that I have of Nikki and Myah are definitely getting burned,* she thought. Somehow, she felt that if she didn't try to extort money from them, then this probably wouldn't have happened. Keisha thought over and over again while she was lying in the hospital bed, that Myah had something to do with her face being slashed. She knew that one way or another, she would get even, but for now, Keisha, who was still looking out of the passenger window as her mother pulled into their driveway, was going to get better physically, while mentally, she was plotting her course for revenge.

Forty-eight hours was the amount of time that every homicide detective gave a case before they started to view it as cold. The first forty-eight hours were critical if you were trying to solve a murder. After that, witnesses disappeared, evidence is misplaced, and even vital information is lost if you took too long. That was the reason why Detective Williamson was so good. He knew how crucial a case could be if handled quickly. He had his team canvas the projects, looking for witnesses, and all evidence was documented and categorized. Nothing slipped through the cracks with Detective Williamson on the scene. Sadell's killer was still out there, just waiting to be caught, and Williamson was going to be the one to bring him in.

Over the weekend, he stayed in his office and went through all of the notes that he and his investigating team wrote down. He even went over the autopsy report of how the victim died. The key witness was a Young man who saw the shooter go into the building with the victim, heard two quick shots, and then the shooter exited the building soon after that.

After talking to the witness himself, Detective Williamson found out that the shooter was a local drug dealer that worked for Dirk Wright, a.k.a. Irk. Now, all the detective had to do was find out the name of the shooter and connect him with Irk, which he knew wasn't going to be easy. He decided that he would bring the witness in to look over some pictures so that he could come up with a positive ID in order to issue an arrest warrant.

It was now one-thirty, and Williamson needed to go home to get some much needed rest. He called it a day and left the precinct to head home. Monday morning, he would bring the witness in. He hoped that he would be able to put a face and name to their killer.

What Williamson didn't know was that by bringing down the killer of the low-level drug dealer, he would also be waist-deep into a much bigger problem later on that would prove to be Detective Williamson's biggest challenge.

Henry was lying on the bunk in his cell, listening to his Walkman radio. He had his eyes closed as he lip-synced the words of the song on the radio. "Back that ass up!" he screamed as Juvenile's song was just about to go off. "Damn! I like that shit there!" he said to no one in particular. He opened his eyes, sat up in the bunk and grabbed a bottle of Coke from off of his desk and took a long swig to quench his thirst.

Henry wasn't tired, he was just frustrated that he had to sit on his stash of dope since his man, Ivan had told him three days ago that he heard that I.A. Officer Roscoe and CO Trustice were paying snitch motherfuckers to set him up or give information about his dealings. He had already figured as much, but actually hearing it from a thorough nigga like Ivan bought the thought to reality.

Henry watched who he talked to and what he said in order not to give anyone any reason to think otherwise. He knew that the staff of crooked CO's would be listening, watching, and trying to figure out what he was doing, but like the book, "48 Laws of Power" that his man, Lil' Gee let him read said, "Know thy enemy better than they know thyself." This was something that he planned on doing. He only had two years left on his sentence, and he wasn't about to let these muthafuckers jack his time any further. He would take a loss if he had to, but he still knew some people in there that he could trust with his stash that would get rid of it for him as well. All he had to do was get in touch with them without bringing too much heat to them. He knew that they would harass anyone he talked to, so he did the next best thing. He had one of his man's people deliver a message to his man, Jay to get him in the chow hall while everyone was around. Henry knew that the obvious was sometimes not so obvious.

After getting out of bed to use the bathroom, Henry walked out of his cell and into the common area where there were people watching TV or playing cards at the many tables that were situated around the "Day Area" as it was called. There were also those who were getting their workout on by doing push-ups, dips and crunches.

Henry looked around, smelling cigarette smoke thick in the air. He pulled out a Newport from his shirt pocket, took out some matches he had in his right pants pocket, and lit it up. He was tired of staying cooped up in his cell all day, so he decided that on the next move, he was going to head out to the rec yard to get some fresh air. Henry knew that once he left, the CO on duty would search his cell, which was clean, because his stash was with someone else. What he was worried about was, if he could get rid of all of it.

He saw that one of the phones was free, so he decided to call Myah to see what she was up to. It's been a minute since he heard from her. The letter that he wrote a week ago was never responded to. As he walked towards the open phone, someone called his name. "Ayo, Henry! Henry!"

the deep voice hollered.

Henry turned around quickly to see who was calling and saw his man, B.J. standing over near the microwaves, waving for him to come over. He took a deep pull on his cigarette and thumped the ashes to the floor as he made his way over towards B.J.

Everyone he made eye contact with nodded their heads or raised their fists to gesture their respect for him. Some of them that were new learned quickly, to respect the O.G. Even though Henry was trying to stay incident-free, he wasn't above making an example out of those that disrespected him.

"Hey, my nigga! What's new with you?" B.J. asked once Henry was close enough to him.

"Ah shit! The same shit, just a different day. What you cookin'?" Henry asked, smelling the aroma that was coming from the microwave.

"Just a little sumptin' sumptin'. Not much. Let me ask you this. You still holding anything for the head?" B.J. asked in a whispered voice.

Henry continued to puff on his cigarette, trying to decide if he could trust B.J., who he has known for about four years now. He thought about telling him who to go to if he was looking to score something, but eventually decided not to. It just wasn't worth the risk. "Nah. I ain't even got nothing for myself. If you find who has some, come holla at me," he stated, taking the focus off of himself.

At that moment, the ten-minute bell rang, indicating it was the move. Henry gave B.J. a pound (handshake) and dipped out of the dorm door that led to the main hallway, and was gone.

While on the yard, Henry met up with some of his homies and kicked the Willie-Bo-Bo for about an hour. After which, he learned that his boy, Ed Ski was in the

SHU (Segregated Housing Unit), staying true to his word by staying quiet and taking the weight. Henry knew that Ed Ski was a thorough type of guy, so once he was released from the hole, Henry planned on blessing him for his silence. Henry also learned that they tacked on another six months to his sentence, which wasn't anything to Ed Ski, considering how long he's been down already. Actually, it was pretty good, since Henry knew that Ed could have received anywhere between two to five additional years, depending on the amount of drugs found on him.

Just as he was about to walk over towards the basketball courts, the PA system came to life. "Hendrick Anderson! Number 80-A-1003, report to your unit! Hendrick Anderson! Report to your unit immediately!"

Henry hated when they screamed his full name, but that didn't bother him. What bothered him was the fact that he didn't know the reason why they were calling him. He did a half lap around the track until he was near the main entrance. He walked up to the officer on duty at the metal detectors, and told him that he was told to return to his unit.

It was going to be another forty minutes before the bell rang for the next move, so the CO on duty had to call in to see if it was okay for Henry to move before it was called. "Control, did you call for Hendrick Anderson?" The CO waited for a response, and after a couple of seconds, the control officer responded back, "Yes, we did. Send him to his unit immediately!" The CO at the metal detector turned to Henry and waved him through, allowing him to go back before the move was called.

"Anderson! Pack up your shit and take it to R&D!" CO Stewart barked at Henry once he stepped into the unit.

"What?" Where the fuck am I going?" Henry asked with a bewildered look on his face.

"I don't know, and I don't give a fuck! Just get your shit and bounce!" Stewart sarcastically answered.

Henry mumbled something to himself while he walked towards his cell. Something was wrong, and as he looked around his cell at all of his property, he decided to find out from someone that would probably know the answer.

Henry went straight to the officer's desk that was located near the front door and asked him to call I.A. Officer Roscoe. "Hey, Stewart, call Officer Roscoe for me. I have to know what's going on," Henry said, standing in the doorway of the little room the CO's called an office.

"What?" Stewart yelled at Henry.

Henry looked at him, and instead of losing his temper with the insolent officer, he simply explained the situation. "Look. I understand that I'm in prison, and I know that the D.O.C. (Department of Corrections) has the right to transfer inmates whenever and wherever. All I'm asking is to call I.A. Officer Roscoe and tell him I need to talk to him. I want to tell him something that's very important." Henry knew that the only reason an inmate talks to I.A. Officer Roscoe is to either snitch, or because they were snitched on.

Stewart didn't particularly like Henry's attitude, but he made the call, and was told by Roscoe to send him over, which he was more than happy to do.

FIVE

Tony woke up early Saturday morning, and looked at Tania's alarm clock on the nightstand next to her bed. "Damn!" he yelled. It was nine-thirty-five, and he had to meet Myah at the Coliseum in Queens by eleven-thirty. He had called her yesterday to make sure she was going to be there, and after talking on the phone for a few minutes, they decided to meet in front at eleven-thirty, which if he didn't get a move on, he would be late.

Last night, while Tha PotHeadz, were performing at Nassau Coliseum, Tony got a visit from someone he thought he would never have the opportunity to ever meet.

"Mr. Moore, I hope that this meeting does not come at a bad time. I know your group is doing a show and all and from the looks of it, they're really putting their thing down." Kevin Lowe said as he leaned over towards Tony in order to be heard over the crowd's loud cheers.

Just as Tony was about to respond, the music stopped, the lights dimmed, and all four members of Tha PotHeadz huddled up in the middle of the stage. Tony knew what they were about to do, perform a crowd favorite, "Intricate Plot."

*"It's the Intricate Plot, I'm watchin' them watch
me. I'm ready for anything whatever it's gotta be.
I keep my enemies close can't let em' murder me.
Gotta try to stay alive and strapped with artillery."*

The music got louder and louder each time they chanted
the chorus until they reached the point where the bass, the
drum, and the synthesizer all blended together to create
the desired effect that they were looking for.

*"Peep the scenario, people plottin', but they
don't hear me though. They're running around in
camouflage trying to get me yo'. The Intricate Plot
is to try and trap the black man, ski-mask way with
the glocks in their right hand..."*

Each member of the group jumped around the stage
getting the crowd amped up and screaming while one of
them said their verse.

Once that person was finished, and the chorus was
sung, Pop, who was the smallest in the group, but one of
the hypest on stage, started to recite his verse.

*"...That plot's kinda scary, yo' I'm dodging my
adversaries. There's no where to hide so then I do
what is necessary..."*

"Ahh! I love this song!" Tony yelled as Pop continued
to energize the crowd with his verse. Kevin Lowe was just
in awe at how the crowd was responding to the group's
stage presence.

"Mr. Moore, I had a conversation with a friend of
mine that told me that I would be making a big mistake if

I didn't take a look at your group." That statement alone had gotten Tony's attention, which made him turn in Kevin's direction to listen to what the CEO of Streetlife Records had to say.

"She also told me that you were looking for someone to sign them to a contract, am I correct?"

'That's correct. I've been with them since the beginning, and I know that they have the potential to sell records. All they need is the opportunity to show their talent."

Kevin liked the way that Tony conducted himself and knew that he was committed and believed in his group 100%.

"As you know, I'm looking to expand my company's fan base, and I believe that after what I've seen here tonight, there's no doubt in my mind that Tha PotHeadz can do just that."

Here's my card. On it, you have all my contact numbers. If you feel that strongly in your group, then give me a call. But before you do, talk it over with everyone and let them know that I'm willing to put everything I have behind them, if they are willing to put in the work."

As if on cue, the crowd gave a loud cheer letting Tony know that his group was finishing up their set. When he heard them all saying, "Thank you! Thank you!" he too grabbed Kevin's extended hand and shook it while at the same time saying the same two words that was bellowing from the speakers.

Later that evening, after everyone had calmed down from the performance that they gave at the Coliseum, Tony took them all to the Tunnel, one of the hottest clubs in the city, to tell them the good news. But before he did, he made sure that Tania was around to also hear what the had to say.

As soon as they entered the club, Tony directed his little entourage towards a group of tables that were just off to the side of the main dance floor. He told the bouncer, whom he knew personally, that he was waiting for one more person and after he described her, the bouncer assured him that he would direct her to where they would be especially after Tony slipped him a Ben Franklin when he gave him a handshake.

While they waited, Tony ordered two bottles of Cristal, not caring about the price. The show that they just finished doing netted them twenty-five hundred dollars, five hundred for each of them. Tony not only made sure that they got their money after the show was over, but that they didn't spend a dime of it while they were in the club. Everything was on him.

"Yo Tony! What's this all about son?" D-dogg asked as he continued to stare at a cute little dark-skinned girl that was on the dance floor with a group of other girls that were just as cute as her.

"Yeah big homie, you've been acting strange ever since we left the Coliseum. On top of that, you've been spending major dough as if there's no tomorrow. What gives?" Pop asked with his eyes glued on Tony.

Just as he was about to explain to them why he had them there, he saw Tania making her way over towards them wearing a form fitting one piece slip-over black dress that hugged every inch of her body and a pair of three inch high-heels that made her strut across the dance floor like she as a stallion.

Tony smiled as he welcomed her over and made room for her to sit down.

"Hey guys! I heard ya'll did your thing out there tonight." Every one of them smiled showing off their gold grills and acting as if they were in junior high with a major crush on their teacher. They all respected and admired Tania ever since the first time they were introduced to her, but the way she was dressed that night, they couldn't stop staring at her curvatrous body, that was wrapped in that thin, clingy material that she called a dress.

"I'm sorry I missed it, but I had to attend a dinner that my job was giving. I would have changed into something a little less formal, but Tony insisted I make it here as quickly as possible." Tania explained with a smile. Jericho looked Tania up and down with lust in his eyes as he said, "You look a'ight to me Ma!" Not knowing the full meaning behind his last statement, Tania just thanked him then turned her attention back to Tony who was now standing up ready to speak.

"A'ight! A'ight! Calm down Casanova." Tony said to Jericho jokingly.

"Now that I have everyone here, I need for ya'll to listen up to what I'm about to say. As ya'll know, Tania has been working real hard trying to find us a company that's willing to take a chance and sign ya'll to a deal." Tania had no idea where Tony was going with this, but as she continued to listen, she remembered talking to Kevin about the group.

"… and as ya'll was on stage performing, I had the pleasure of meeting Mr. Kevin Lowe, CEO and President of Streetlife Records. Actually, he introduced himself to me." Everyone's jaws literally dropped because they knew who Kevin Lowe was and the fact that he was at their show was a big deal.

"He informed me that after talking to a special friend of his." When Tony said that, he looked over in Tania's direction and smiled.

"Who told him that he would be making a big mistake if he didn't at least check ya'll out. So as ya'll was on stage rappin', one of my favorite songs, ya'll were actually giving Kevin Lowe a demo of what ya'll could truly do. To make a long story short, he liked what he heard and saw. He offered ya'll a record deal if ya'll want to take it." Before Tony could say another word, Jericho, Pop, D-dogg, and E-money all jumped up and hugged each other as if they had just won the lottery.

But before they got too out of control, Tony also added, "That special friend that told him about ya'll was this lovely lady right here. So, I think ya'll owe her…" just as before; they didn't even give him a chance to finish before they all came over and hugged Tania who acted as if she didn't do anything big.

Once they were through congratulating and thanking Tony and Tania, the group partied and mingled with the crowd leaving Tony and Tania all alone.

"Well Ms. Thang. I guess I owe you a dinner huh?"

"Nope! But I will settle for you taking me home and granting me three little wishes." Tania said seductively as Tony leaned in for a deep passionate kiss.

They stayed at the Tunnel for three hours partying before Tony left with Tania to do some celebrating of their own. The rest of the night was a blur.

"Hmmm! And where do you think you're going?" Tania asked when she felt Tony getting out of bed.

They were in her spacious one bedroom apartment in Brooklyn that overlooked the magnificent skyline of New York City. She wanted to quit her job with Roc-a-fella Records in order to help Tony manage his group. She was going to help them get all that they deserved, since she knew how the music industry operated.

"I have to meet someone in Queens today," Tony said as he walked around her bedroom, trying to find his black tank top that he took off during the night.

Even though Tania wasn't his girl—or wasn't as of yet—she still felt the feelings of someone that was in a committed relationship. Being that they were just "friends with benefits", she knew it was wrong for her to act like a jealous girlfriend, but she liked Tony very much, and it was hard for her not to. "I hope it's not another woman!" she said jokingly as she sat up on her elbows with the sheets around her stomach, exposing her perfect 34-B cups.

Tony smiled, knowing that she was dead serious, even though she was smiling. He really liked the relationship that they had. She made him laugh, which wasn't easy for anyone to do. They made a good couple, but Tony didn't want to rush anything.

On the other hand, Tania wanted to settle down with someone. She was tired of the dating game, and of all the immature men that were intimidated by her because she was an independent woman. Tony was different. He had goals, and he treated her as his equal, which she wasn't used to, when she was around other brothers she dated. Their relationship was simple, yet both were content. She didn't want to complicate things because of her jealousy, but Tony knew that was a sign of her showing weakness.

Under Tania's strong shell was a woman that had emotions, and Tony welcomed the vulnerability. Even though he didn't have to justify his actions to her, he wanted to make sure that she knew that she had nothing to worry about. "Do I detect someone being a little possessive up in here?" he jokingly asked while putting on his black Timberland boots.

Tania folded her arms over her chest and pretended to pout, as she turned away from him when he came over towards her. "Oh yeah? Well maybe I am. Do I need to be?"

"Damn, girl! You make a brother feel real special by

the way you're questioning me," Tony shot back as he leaned over to give her a kiss on the cheek.

When she felt his lips on her face, she quickly turned around in order for him to kiss her on her lips. Tony planted a soft, wet kiss on her lips once he realized what she was trying to do. Then, he pulled back just in time before she had the chance to grab and pull him onto the bed.

That's not fair! You're just gonna up and leave a sista in this condition by herself?" She pulled the sheets that were covering her medium built frame to reveal all of her splender and glory that Tony was so fond of.

He did a double take, while his dick came to life inside of his jeans. He looked at his watch, and it read five minutes to ten. He calculated in his head just how long it would take him to get to the Coliseum from where he was, and after about two seconds, he figured that he had just enough time to break Tania off a little something before he left. "Nah, I'm not gonna leave you like that!" he replied as he undid his jeans, kicked off his boots and crawled in bed with her.

Tania smiled, and knew that Tony was definitely a keeper, for sure!

Myah had just finished in the bathroom and was just about to sit down at her vanity when she heard her cell phone ringing on her bed. She looked at her clock on the desk and saw that it was only ten-twelve. "Who tha fuck... hello!" she answered in a sarcastic tone of voice.

"Damn, girl! Why you answering the phone like that?" Nikki asked as she tried to figure out the mood that Myah was in.

"Oh, hey, Nikki. I was just trying to get ready so that

I could meet someone."

Nikki wanted to be nosy, and Myah knew it. "Who ya meeting?" Nikki asked in an inquisitive voice.

"Nun-ya!"

"Nun-ya? Who's that?"

"None of ya damn business, girl!" Myah replied, laughing out loud because Nikki actually fell for that old trick.

"That wasn't funny, Myah!" Nikki screamed, trying to get Myah's attention.

"Yeah, it was. How could you fall for that old shit, Nik?"

"What ever-r-r-r! Are you really meeting someone?" she asked once again.

This time, Myah gave in. "Yeah. Remember that guy I gave my cell number to at the club on my birthday before we left to go to my apartment?"

"Yeah," Nikki answered.

"Well, that was my mom's boyfriend before she died. He wants to talk to me at the mall in Queens—"

Before Myah could finish, Nikki jumped in. "Can I come? I need to pick up some things anyway."

"Nah, girl, not this time. I need to talk to him *alone*," Myah stressed strongly, suggesting that she didn't want any company.

Nikki made a face once she heard the way Myah emphasized the word "alone". "Well, I'm sorry for asking!" she sarcastically said in retaliation.

Myah looked in the mirror of her vanity and smiled. She knew that her friend was salty, but she had to stay firm. "I have to get dressed, Nik. Let me call you back once I'm on the road, okay?"

"Yeah, a'ight. Make sure you do that!" Nikki replied as she closed her phone and cut off the connection.

Myah heard the click, pulled the phone away from her ear and made a face of disappointment. She couldn't believe that Nikki hung up on her. "I know she didn't!" she said aloud while closing her phone.

After Myah fixed her hair and applied the finishing touches to her makeup, she then walked over to her closet in her matching white satin Victoria's Secret bra and panties set to pick out a nice sexy outfit to wear. "I need something sexy, but not too revealing," she said to herself out loud as she picked through various tight fitting jeans she had hanging up in her closet. She decided to wear a pair of Tommy Girl jeans that would hug her hips and accentuate her voluptuous ass. She then found a red Tommy Hilfiger wife-beater shirt that would also fit tight to show off her ample chest and flat stomach. "Yeah, this will do it!"

When she was finished getting dressed, she looked in her full-length mirror on the back of her door, and was satisfied with what she had picked out. Her red, white and blue Tommy Hilfiger sneakers matched her outfit perfectly.

Myah was ready to leave. She looked at her Fossil watch with the red and blue leather band, and saw that it was now ten-forty-three. "Damn! I have to get out of here!" she said to herself as she grabbed her black leather Coach bag from off her dresser and proceeded to walk out of her room. Before she hit the light switch, she took one last look at herself and said, "Damn, girl! You're looking good!" Then, she flipped the switch and left to meet Tony.

Tony was on the train to Jamaica, Queens, heading to the Coliseum. He was wearing a pair of light tan Pelle-Pelle jeans with a pair of buckskin Tims to match. His brown Pelle-Pelle pullover shirt set off his jeans perfectly, while he let his dreads hang loosely around his face. The train pulled into the station, and Tony walked down the platform until he reached the main stairway that led to Jamaica Avenue. He was greeted by the bright sunlight, which made him squint his eyes. He pulled out his gold framed Cartier sunglasses, placed them over his eyes.

The streets were crowded with people coming and going, cars honking their horns, and music was blasting everywhere. It was a nice sunny day in New York, and Tony blended in with the crowd as he walked the few blocks towards the Coliseum. It was only eleven-twenty. He had ten minutes to kill before he was to meet up with Myah, so he did some window shopping to waste the time. Beautiful women were walking around in their tight clothing, showing off their bodies, and a few even smiled as they passed him by. With his glasses on, he was able to look at their asses as they strolled along the avenue, going from one store to the next.

Tony looked at his Movado watch and saw that he had only a few minutes more before Myah was to meet him. He was a little nervous. He really didn't know what to expect from the meeting, but he had to know how she was doing, especially since the death of her mother. As he was standing in front of the Coliseum, he heard a female voice call out his name. "Tony! To-o-o-ny!"

Myah raced down Southern State Parkway towards Queens with her system thumping. She was in another world as she listened to Mobb Deep's "Murder Muzic" CD: "...*It's real-l-l-l hip-hop, hip-hop*..." She looked at her clock in the dashboard and saw that she had about an hour to get there. Her speedometer read sixty-eight mph, while she traveled in the fast lane. Traffic was moving along, so she knew that she would make it in time. Once she reached the Jamaica Avenue exit, it was going on eleven-fifteen. She had to find a parking spot as close to the Coliseum as possible.

The sun was shining brightly, which made her car sparkle.

The traffic on the avenue was moving slowly, which added to Myah's frustration. While she was at a red light, she rolled the window down to feel the light breeze that was blowing. Just as she was about to move, she saw a car that was about to pull out of its parking spot. She put on her right blinker and let the car pull out. Once it was on the street, she pulled into the spot and cut the engine off. She was about three blocks from the Coliseum, so she knew that she got lucky. She waited for a break in the traffic, then opened her door to get out.

Once she was out and standing safely on the sidewalk, she pressed her key chain to activate the car's alarm system. She looked at her watch and saw that she had about five minutes left, so she quickly walked down the congested block until she spotted Tony looking around in front of the Coliseum's entrance. She called his name just loud enough for him to hear. "Tony! To-o-o-ny!"

Myah and Tony walked and talked for about two hours, learning everything about each other and what the other had been up to in the last twelve years. Myah learned more about her mother and about that fatal night that her mother was killed, which brought tears to her eyes.

Tony learned a great deal about Myah, and what she's been doing since that day she was taken away. What he didn't know was that Myah harbored strong feelings of revenge. She offered Tony a ride back to his apartment, which he declined. She told him that she vowed years ago after she learned the truth, that she would bring justice to her mother's death.

Tony didn't think about it then, but as he hopped back on the train to head home, he realized that Myah had an agenda, and it included get-back. He promised himself that day that he would watch out for her and protect her from making a terrible mistake. After finally finding her, he already lost one girl to a monster, so he wasn't about to let it happen again.

SIX

With all of the things that were going on in Myah's life, she still managed to keep control of everything, except what was going on with her pen pal, Hendrick. As she sat in her bedroom in her aunt and uncle's house, she wondered why she hasn't received any mail from him yet. "What tha fuck is going on with him? He hasn't called or wrote in two weeks," she said out loud to herself. She wanted to find out the reason why, so she decided to pick up the phone and call the prison he was in. "Hello, I'm calling to check on the status of an inmate there."

"And what is the inmate's name and D.O.C. number?" the beautiful dark skinned young woman asked.

Myah read off Hendrick's name and number from an envelope she had received from him about a week and a half ago. "His name is Hendrick Anderson, number 89-A-1003."

The young woman punched his name and number into the computer she had in front of her, and once his profile came up, she said, "That inmate was transferred to Danamora (Clinton Correctional Facility) in Clinton, New York about a week ago. Is that all, Miss?"

Myah was shocked. He never told her he was transferring. "Yes, that's all. Thank you," she added before hanging up the phone. She sat back on her bed and thought about her next move. She wanted to call up there, but she knew that they wouldn't let her talk to him. Then, she thought about the college she was going to be attending and how close it was to Clinton, New York. "Ahhh! I'll be able to visit now, since it's right near the school. I can surprise his ass with a visit," she said to herself. "Yeah! He'll be surprised to see me, I bet!" She laid in her bed and fell asleep with that thought on her mind, as she dreamt of how she came to find out about Hendrick Anderson:

Jasmine, who has been friends with Myah since junior high school, was looking for her cousin, Ricky, who was sent to a medium security prison in Upstate New York, came across a site on the internet that listed the prisons and inmates' names listed in alphabetical order. Myah saw Hendrick's name on that, and it brought back a flood of memories that weren't pleasant. The look on her face was one of total shock, which wasn't lost on the others who were next to her.

"Myah, what's wrong? You look like you saw a ghost," Christine asked.

Myah's thoughts went back to when she was five-years-old, the same day that she heard her mother yelling at who she thought was Tony, but later learned was someone that she had never seen before that day. The scar on his face was what triggered all of the memories that she had suppressed for so long. As she continued to look at his picture and the brief bio that they gave on the inmate, she began to visualize all of the things that she wanted to do to him for taking away the one person that meant the most to her; her mother. Hendrick Anderson was the name he was listed under at Elmira State Penitentiary where he was incarcerated.

Myah snapped out of her trance, grabbed a pen from off the desk, along with a piece of yellow stationary paper, and wrote down the name and address of Hendrick Anderson.

"Damn, girl! You think he's that cute, huh?" Nikki asked as she continued to look at the picture on the screen, trying to figure out what was so appealing about him.

"He's not that cute!" Jasmine added as she scrunched her face up in disgust.

Myah ignored them all, until she was finished writing. She knew that she couldn't let them know who she thought he was, so she quickly thought up a good story. "Please! I know you heifers think he's cute in a rough looking way."

They all laughed out loud as Jasmine continued to scroll down the Web Page to find her cousin, Ricky's address.

Henry was sent to Danamora Penitentiary, in Clinton, New York. Since I.A. Officer Roscoe couldn't force his hand or get anyone to give information on him, he decided to unload him off on another facility to deal with. Henry went from a medium security facility to a maximum security facility as a form of punishment. But, what I.A. Officer Roscoe didn't know was that Henry had friends everywhere he went, so no matter where they put him, he was still going to be treated as an influential figure from the 'hood.

Back on Long Island, Myah and Nikki were making

plans for the prom that was just a week away. They were at Nikki's house in the kitchen, looking through the phone book, trying to find a Limousine service with a reasonable price.

"Myah, why can't we just use one of my father's Limo's?" Nikki asked from across the wooden kitchen island that was stationed right in the center of the spacious kitchen.

Myah looked up from the Yellow Pages that was in front of her, and replied, "'Cause people already know what your father's Limos look like. That's why!"

"It wouldn't cost us anything, and we wouldn't have to worry about getting it back by a certain time," Nikki shot back, trying to get Myah to understand.

Myah didn't care about paying for the Limo or how long they would have it. All she cared about was stepping out of something extravagant. "Nik, do you want your last time around these people to be the same? Or do you want them to remember you for what you came to the prom in, and how you left? You decide, then holla at me, a'ight?" Myah definitely wasn't worried about the price. Irk already promised to foot the bill, so all she had to do was find one, which was proving to be more difficult than it seemed.

Back in the Bronx, Detective Williamson had questioned a witness about the murder of Sadell Jones, and learned that the shooter was a young hitman named Byron Pitts, a.k.a. Young Bizarini. After issuing an arrest warrant for him, Detective Williamson was informed by one of the officers that knew the projects well, that it was common knowledge that Sadell worked for Dirk Wright.

The detective was fully aware of this information, but what he didn't know was that the shooter was also linked to Mr. Wright as well. Now, it didn't take a rocket scientist to figure out that Dirk Wright was in the middle, or possibly the one that gave the order for the hit. Williamson made it his business to bring "Irk" and his drug empire down by any means necessary.

Just as he was about to pick up his phone, a thought suddenly hit him. Myah Johnson was liked to Dirk Wright, and by being so, he would have to proceed with caution until he knew the exact extent of their relationship. *Damn! I know she's a good kid, but what possible reason would she need him for?* Williamson thought to himself as he replaced the receiver back on its cradle.

The detective would have to reevaluate his next move if he was to bring Irk down without bringing Myah down along with him.

"Ayo, Irk, you know that five-O got your boy... what's his name...? Oh, yeah, Young Bizarini. It's all over the news right now," Big Zo said while they were pulling up into the Soundview Projects. He had forgotten all about what he saw on TV just before he picked Irk up from one of his spots, but as he was entering the projects, something triggered his memory.

Irk sat in the passenger seat of his Benz 600, cool, calm, and collected. It looked as if he didn't care or didn't hear what his trusted lieutenant was saying.

Zo looked over towards him once he parked the car in the parking spot in front of the building that they were about to enter. After the engine was cut off, Irk said, without looking in Zo's direction, "I heard about it. One of the young gunz around the way hit me up on the three-way and told me about it." Somehow, Irk didn't look too fazed about the bad news. That was because he knew that Young Bizarini was good at doing a disappearing act. If he heard about the all points bulletin, then he knew that Bizarini was already two steps ahead of everybody else.

"What you wanna do?" Zo asked before he was about to step out of the car.

"It's already taken care of," Irk responded before he opened the door. He stepped out, leaving Zo inside wondering if his man was losing it because of how he was acting. But what Big Zo didn't know was that Irk had already contacted Young Bizarini and told him to meet Taz at the spot in Brooklyn to get some money in order for him to disappear.

Taz, who was an up and coming hitman himself, had been working for Irk since he was seventeen. Now at the age of twenty-three, he was in charge of Irk's Brooklyn operation, which was bringing in close to a million a week. Irk had called him on his cell phone and told him that Young Bizarini was coming to see him, and for him to take care of the problem that could easily bring all of them down. Taz heard about the police looking into the murder of one of his workers, and he knew that Young Bizarini was the shooter, so when Irk gave him the green light, he was prepared to do what was needed.

Knowing that Bizarini would know a setup when he saw one, Taz had to play it off as if he was giving him some disappearing money. Once Bizarini arrived, Taz handed him a duffel bag that contained fifty-thousand-dollars, and keys to a blue '92 Audi 5000, which he could use to get out of the city with.

Bizarini never suspected that Taz would do him any harm, since they had been working together ever since he came to Irk. But, before he had a chance to make it to the car with the bag, Taz pulled out his .22 and shot him four times in the back of the head at close range, leaving him lying next to the Audi, which he had registered in a crack head's name.

Taz looked around before picking up the bag of money, and walked off down the dark street, heading to his '97 Chevy Suburban that he had parked in a parking lot less than an hour before.

SEVEN

The murder of Sadell was never solved, nor was the murder of Young Bizarini, who was found in a parking lot, face down with four shots to his head. Detective Williamson knew in his heart that both murders were connected to Irk somehow, but proving that theory was another story.

Weeks passed without another incident, which left the veteran detective without closure. He was determined now more than ever to bring Irk down, even if that meant jeopardizing all that he worked so hard for.

Tony's group, Tha PotHeadz, with their new contract with Streetlife Records, was now in the studio, recording their first album, which was slated to go platinum with all of the promotion and backing that they were getting.

Tony and Tania's relationship was becoming more of an intimate one than a business one. Tania moved in with Tony after they learned that she was pregnant.

Myah and Nikki went to their prom with Irk and one of his friends. Irk paid for everything, which left Nikki wondering if her and Myah's friendship was coming to an end. Since they were both heading off to college in three months, Nikki was now trying to find out about being on her own. The love that she had for Myah was proving to be more difficult to let go of. After all they've been through, she knew she couldn't just let go without knowing exactly where they stood.

Myah had a lot on her plate, especially since she was becoming more attached to Irk. She knew that she had to be stronger mentally if what she was planning to do was to work. Weakness was something she wasn't going to have if she was to carry out all of the things that she had decided to do. Hendrick had to believe that she was there for him, and with his parole coming soon, she knew that she had to start focusing more on him than on what was going on with Irk.

Since graduation was now only a week away, she and Nikki's lives were going to change, one way or another. Myah wanted to spend her last couple of months with her best friend, but with all that was going on with her, Irk and Hendrick, she knew she would be spreading herself thin.

Clinton Correctional Facility, known as Danamora, was a place that the State of New York sent their worst of the worst. The imposing fifty-foot wall that surrounded the prison was enough to scare anyone that saw it. The prison itself, which was a fortress, was situated dead smack in the middle of the town. Almost everyone in the immediate area worked there, from the correctional officers down to the maintenance crew that took care of the day-to-day operations of the massive facility.

Henry heard many scary stories about the place, but he never thought that he would actually be an occupant himself. After arriving at Danamora a month ago, he was now familiar with the layout and its occupants. He was quickly becoming "the man to know", since most of the big wigs there respected his hustle and the way he moved. A couple of so-called tough guys tried him, but they quickly found out that Henry was not to be fucked with. He was good with his hands since he was a fourth-degree black belt. The little scuffles that he got himself into were just that, and really didn't do much to hurt his status. In fact, they probably made him someone to fear even more.

Henry cliqued up with those who basically ran the joint, which gave him some clout with the officers as well. What I.A. Officer Roscoe thought he sent Henry to Danamora for, actually backfired on him. It only gave Henry more of a name amongst the worst of the worst.

As he was sitting around in his cell, waiting for chow to be called, he was flipping through an *XXL* magazine, when he came across an article about a group of four kids from his 'hood, who were quickly becoming known as the next ONYX. While he read the article, he looked at the picture that the magazine had taken of the group, and of their manager, who Henry thought he recognized from somewhere. "Damn! Son looks mad familiar!" he said as he continued to read.

Henry thought for a second, trying to remember where he knew the manager from, but before he could figure it out, his man, Big Swope came into his cell to see if he was going to chow. "Ayo, Hen-Dog, you going to chow when they call it?" Big Swope asked as he walked further in.

Henry looked up from the magazine and said, "Hell yeah! I'm hungry as a muthafucka! I didn't eat any of that shit they had for lunch today."

Big Swope noticed the *XXL* magazine with Eve on the cover, and reached out for it. "Is that the new one?"

"Yeah, it's Jay's. He just got it yesterday."

Henry gave it to him with the page of the article he was reading face up. Once Swope saw it, he said something that made Henry look up. "Oh, that's that nigga that's got that new group, Tha PotHeadz. Have you heard their new shit yet?"

"Nah. All I know is that those niggas are from around my 'hood," Henry stated with some pride in his voice.

"Those niggas are blowing tha fuck up right now. I like their shit, especially that video." Swope started singing part of their song to see if Henry had heard it:

"This is a letter to my man, explaining it all.
I kept it real with you, nigga, when I took the fall.
I hope you're taking care of business while you're
out there, Black,
'Cause when I hit the streets, you know
I'm coming for that."

Henry listened as Swope continued, and felt that the song had some truth to it. Since he was about to be paroled in another year or so, he felt that people out there owed him for keeping his mouth shut. "A lot of muthafuckas are eating real good out there, and I plan on collecting once I hit the bricks," Henry stated, more to himself than to his man.

"Just don't forget about ya boy," Big Swope responded. Swope was about to go home within the next year. He was just finishing up a three to six year bid for attempted murder, which he had knocked down to an assault charge. He was good peoples, and Henry planned on looking out for him when they touched down.

The chow bell rang, which made Swope stop in mid-sentence. Henry got up off of his bunk, placed the *XXL* magazine under his pillow, walked towards his door and left his cell to go with his man to chow.

EIGHT

Henry finally received the one letter that he'd been waiting on for almost a month now. It has been a few months since he saw the Parole Board, and in his mind, it went pretty well. His hopes were high, but he also knew that they could only hit him another year at the most.

He opened the envelope with the Parole Board Commissioner's return address on it, and pulled out the single sheet of paper that was in it. He knew even before reading it that it was good news. Normally, if it was a rejection letter, the envelope would have been thicker, with appeal papers in it, so feeling thinness of the letter, Henry already knew what it was. He unfolded the paper to read it. His stomach was in knots with the anticipation of the good news:

Dear Mr. Anderson:

You have been granted parole, with the stipulation that you complete a pre-release program within the next two weeks from the date of this letter.

Upon your release, you will be required to report to your parole officer within seventy-two hours. Failing to do so will result in an immediate violation, in which you will be ordered back to complete the remainder of your sentence.

Congratulations, and good luck!

> *Sincerely,*
> *Mr. Thorton*
> *Parole Board Commissioner*

Henry re-read the letter twice more just to make sure he read it right the first time. A smile formed on his face as he placed the letter, along with the envelope, on his bunk. He stood up, and without thinking, yelled, "Hell yeah!" at the top of his lungs.

"Shut tha fuck up!" someone screamed down the tier from him.

Normally, Henry would have said something, but he was feeling too good to even respond. Now, he was ready to start preparing for the streets. Just as he was doing a mental inventory of what he wanted to do first, Myah popped into his head. "Damn! I'll be able to finally tap that young phat ass!" he stated to himself. He walked over to his mirror and took a long hard look at himself. "They better be ready out there! Hen-Dog is back! They've been eating long enough without me, so now it's time for me to get mine." Henry smiled, then turned to walk out of the cell, leaving the letter and envelope on his bunk, face down.

Myah was two months into her freshman year, and she was having the time of her life. Between partying and meeting all different types of people from all over, she couldn't decide which was more exciting. With the schoolwork taken care of, at least for now, she had time to relax a little before going to the cafeteria to get something to eat for dinner.

Since her roommate, Anessa was still in class until three-thirty, Myah had the room to herself, so she kicked off her shoes, jumped on her bed, and decided to listen to some music while she rested. She grabbed the remote to her stereo, pushed the button for the CD changer, and pressed selection #4 to hear Avante's album. While the album played, she closed her eyes and dozed off. When she awoke, Anessa was sitting at her desk, playing on the computer that the school gave to each student, free of charge. It was a small gift, considering the amount that the parents had to pay each year for their child's tuition.

Clarkson University was one of the best engineering schools in the country, and Myah was proud to be a student. Even though she was in her freshman year, she still wanted to keep her GPA around a 3.0 or better.

Without the students from Potsdam College and Clarkson University, the town of Potsdam held about two thousand people, if that. But when school was in session, that number grew to about twenty-five thousand or more, easily. The bars, clubs and eateries loved the business that the students brought in, so they catered specially to them. Once the summertime came and all of the students left — besides the ones that stayed to take summer classes — the town turned back into "Hicksville, USA", a virtual ghost town to say the least. Myah hadn't experienced that yet, but what she did see was all of the excitement that the town had to offer.

It was a Thursday afternoon, and most of the students were preparing to head downtown to enjoy the nightlife. Myah was no exception. Once Anessa saw that she was awake, she stopped what she was doing and turned her attention to Myah. "Hey, sleepy head," she said as she logged off of her computer.

Myah looked around for her clock that was on her desk and saw that it read five-thirty-eight. "When did you get in?" she asked, after clearing her throat.

"I came in around four and saw that you were asleep with the music playing, so I cut the stereo off and logged onto the computer to chat with my friend, Nicole, from home."

Anessa was a pretty, petite young thing that stood about five-one, and weighed no more than a hundred pounds soaking wet. Guys were going crazy over her coffee and cream complexion, long black curly hair, and hazel-brown eyes. Not to mention, that she had a small waist and curvy ass with a nice set of B-cup tits to match her already well-proportioned frame. All in all, she was a cutie, but in her own eyes, she was just an average girl from Burlington, Vermont.

Myah knew after meeting her that Anessa was a little green, meaning she was a bit naïve when it came to certain things; boys being one of them. At eighteen years old, Anessa only had one boyfriend, and they'd been going out since junior high. Even though she's away from home, Anessa still keeps in touch with her friends and family via the Internet or cell phone regularly.

As Anessa continued to talk, Myah's stomach

growled, indicating that she had to get something to eat, and fast. "Did you eat yet?" she asked Anessa as she got out of bed to put her sneakers on.

Myah was wearing a pair of loose fitting black denim Parasuco jeans, with a white, three-buttoned pullover rugby shirt. Her hair was a mess since she had just woken up, but once she brushed it out and put it in a ponytail, it looked good. Her white and blue AirMax sneakers were sitting next to her bed where she left them, so all she had to do was slip them on. She went to her dresser, grabbed her shower bag containing her toiletries, and excused herself as she opened up their room door to head to the bathroom they shared with the other women on the floor.

Their dorm was an eight floor coed building. Each floor consisted of either all males or all females. There weren't any floors that had both. Every level had a common bathroom for the residents on that floor to share. Since Myah was a freshman, she was required to spend her first year on campus. But after that year, she could move to another dorm off campus, which she planned to do as soon as her second semester was over.

While Myah was in the bathroom brushing her teeth, her phone rang in her room, leaving Anessa to answer it. "Hello-o-o!"

"Yeah, who's this?" the voice on the other end asked.

"Who's this?" Anessa shot back with a little sarcasm in her voice. She hated it when people called and asked that question.

"A'ight, shawty. I'ma let that slide for now, but don't let it happen again, a'ight?" the voice stated with confidence.

Anessa didn't know who it was, but whoever it was, was definitely pissing her off, big time. "Listen. I don't know who this is, nor do I care to. But when you call my

phone asking me who I am, then give me warnings as if
you're the president or something, I'ma be sarcastic like
a muthafucka! So, once again, *Who is this, and who do you
want to talk to?"*
Henry was feeling shawty's style. He liked her
attitude. He smiled as he thought about what she just said,
and decided to give up. "My bad, baby girl. I'm looking
for Myah. Is she in?"
Anessa knew that he had to be from New York by
the way he talked. It seemed that everyone she met either
called her "shawty" or "baby girl". It didn't bother her,
but it did make her smile. "Now, that's more like it. No,
she's not here right now, but she should be back in... oh,
wait a minute, she just walked in." Anessa motioned for
Myah to take the phone, and as she handed it to her, Myah
mouthed, "Who is it?"
"I don't know. He won't say his name," Anessa
whispered back.
Myah put the phone to her ear, and in a low voice
said, "Hello."
"Yeah, baby girl. What's up?"
Myah's eyes rolled as she sat on her bed to talk to
Henry. She hadn't heard from him in about a week, and
the last time she went to visit him, he acted like he was
mad with her because she wouldn't do what he wanted.
She wasn't about to jeopardize herself just to please him, so
when she adamantly refused to bring drugs in for him, he
made it known that he was clearly upset with her decision.
When she left, she had to figure out whether she wanted
to continue what she planned on doing, or let it go. In the
end, she decided to keep on track and accomplish what
she set out to do when she first started.
"Hey, baby, I missed you! Why haven't you called
me?" Myah played it off for his benefit. She really couldn't

have cared less if he called her or not, but in order for what she wanted to do, she had to make him believe that she was really excited to hear from him. "Are you still upset with me, baby?" she asked in her sweetest voice.

Anessa looked at Myah with a suspicious eye and smiled.

Henry loved the way Myah sounded. His dick got hard instantly as she continued to pour it on.

"I was worried. I was going to come up to see you, but I didn't want to be turned away because you were mad at me." Myah knew that he would feel as if he had broken her down, but she had to keep pretending if she wanted him to trust her. "Are you alright? I felt bad about—"

"Whoa, whoa, whoa, baby girl! Everything's cool. I'm not mad with you. In fact, I've been missing your fine ass. When are you coming to visit me again?" he asked as he started to stroke his dick through his baggy green khaki pants.

"Well, I have to go back home this weekend. I can try to come up on Sunday when I get back." Myah was lying through her teeth. She planned on visiting Nikki at her school, which was only ten minutes away. They planned on going to Nikki's school's homecoming game, but she couldn't tell him that.

Anessa motioned to Myah that she was going out, then opened the door and left. Since she was alone in the room, Myah decided to have some fun with his ass. "Hey, baby, whatcha doin' right now?"

"Standing at this phone, talking to you." Henry knew what she was trying to do by the way her voice got soft and seductive, so he let her go on.

"You know what?"

"What?" Henry shot back as he looked around to make sure he was alone.

"I'm laying on my bed with my hands on my tits, thinking about your lips on them. Hmmmm!"

Henry continued to stroke himself as he listened.

"What do you want me to do now?" she asked while looking in the mirror at herself, laughing quietly.

"You know what I want you to do. Play with that pussy for daddy!"

"You have to get me wet first."

"Well, imagine me kissing down your stomach as you spread those thick thighs of your's apart in order for me to lick your pussy lips." The more he talked, the faster he stroked.

"Hmmm, yeah, that'll work. Don't forget the clit, baby. Suck it! Suck it too!" Myah added seductively. With him talking like that, she couldn't front any longer. She laid on her bed and decided to play with herself, since it's been a minute since she's had a good nut.

Henry started to breathe harder as he became more excited by her sexy voice. He couldn't wait to sink his dick into her wet pussy once he got out. *It won't be long!* he thought to himself as he continued to listen to her talk nasty.

"How many fingers do you want me to put in there?"

"How many do you have in there now?"

"Just one," she answered as she unbuttoned her jeans and placed a finger in her pussy.

"Well, put two in now."

"Ahhh! It's so wet, baby! Damn! I wish you were here right now!"

"Pop it for me. Put the phone down there and pop that pussy for daddy!" Henry demanded.

Myah placed the phone down near her pussy and moved her fingers in and out very quickly in order for Henry to hear the sloshing sounds. She rubbed her finger against her clitoris, and felt herself about to cum. She couldn't hold back any longer and let it all go without even thinking. "Ahhh! Ohhh! Ohhh yeah!"

Henry couldn't stand another second. He too came in his hand. "Damnit!" he said into the phone as his nut sprayed against his hand and the inside of his pants.

"You okay, baby?" Myah asked after putting the phone back to her ear and hearing him cursing.

Henry couldn't believe it. He fucked up the front of his pants. Now he would have to go and change before going out to the recreation yard. "Yeah, yeah, yeah. I just made a mess on myself, that's all."

Myah laughed out loud as she grabbed her box of tissues from off her dresser to clean up. "Well, if it's worth anything, I made a mess too!"

They both laughed as Myah heard someone outside her door. She quickly buttoned up her jeans and pretended to be just sitting on her bed and talking on the phone as the door began to open up.

NINE

Irk was laying on his California king size motionless waterbed, getting his dick sucked by a pretty pecan brown sister that he had met at the club last night, when his phone rang. He let it ring three more times before he decided to pick it up. "Hello!" he answered as the young girl, who couldn't have been any older than twenty, stopped what she was doing to allow him to talk freely.

"Hey, baby! What's up?"

As soon as Irk heard Myah's voice, he quickly motioned for the young girl to go into the other room. His voice changed from that of irritation to something of surprise.

The voice change wasn't lost on the young girl. She knew that she was just there for pleasure, which wasn't a problem for her since Irk was paying her for her time. She got up off the bed, bent over to pick up the towel that she left there before climbing into bed that morning, and gave Irk a full view of her shaved pussy and went out the door to use the bathroom.

Once she was out of earshot, Irk continued to talk. "I'm sorry, I just got up. I stayed out with the fellas until about three this morning. What's up? Everything a'ight up there in College-ville, USA?"

Myah wasn't stupid, nor did she believe that her man was back in the Bronx nine hours away being an angel. She knew he had bitches that he could fuck with no strings attached, but as long as she wasn't disrespected, it was all good. "Everything's cool. I was just calling to see when you were coming up to visit me. I know you miss your kitty cat, right?"

Irk went to visit Myah at least once a week, and whenever he did, she made sure that she laid it down for her man. The things she did to him were things that no one else could possibly do. She was a lady in the streets, but with her man, she was a freak in the sheets, and Irk knew it. He was sprung, no doubt, but he never would let her know that.

Irk loved the way Myah talked when it came to sex. Her sexy tone of voice made his dick hard instantly. "You know I've missed my kitty cat," he answered back.

"Then, when are you coming to take care of business?" Myah quickly shot back at him.

Just as he was about to answer her question, the young girl opened his bedroom door and quietly walked in to grab her panties that were lying on the floor next to the bed. Before she had a chance to sneak out, Irk hit the bed to get her attention. Once she turned around, he motioned for her to be quiet, and come back to bed to finish what she had been doing. She smiled after seeing how hard he was, and dropped everything, climbed back into bed between his legs, and proceeded to finish the job of getting him off.

Irk cleared his throat and said, "Well, I won't be able to make it up this weekend only because I have to go into Brooklyn to pick up some work. If you're free on Tuesday, then I'll head up there then."

Myah was relieved that she didn't have to lie to him. She thought for a second about what she had to do on Tuesday, and told him that she was free, since all of her classes would be over by one. "That'll be good. You know that I'm disappointed, don't you?" "Yeah, I know. But when I get there Tuesday, I'll definitely make it up to you. I promise." "You better! I'm really missing my 'Snickers'!" That was the name she gave his dick since it was big, packed with nuts, and really satisfying.

Irk laughed out loud, which made the young girl stop sucking, since his sudden outburst almost caused her to gag. He looked down at her, touched the top of her head and held it until she continued her slow sucking and caressing of his dick. Once she had her rhythm back to where he liked it, he went back to talking to Myah. "And you know he misses you too."

Irk felt himself reaching that point, so before he really got into it, he decided to cut the phone conversation short. "Hey, princess, let me call you back. I have to use the bathroom, take a shower, and then get dressed before Big Zo picks me up. I'll give you a call once I'm back here, okay?"

"A'ight, but make sure you call me. I hate it when you go to cop. I just don't trust any of those Dominicans you deal with."

"No need to worry your pretty little head about me. You know I'm well protected at all times." Which was true. At any given time, Irk had about five men with him whenever he rolled anywhere.

"Love ya!" Myah shouted.

"I love you too, princess," Irk replied before he hung up the phone. He got off just in time, because he couldn't hold back any longer as he let off a week's worth of nut into the young girl's pretty mouth. She did her best to swallow it all, but it was just too much, as Irk pumped his dick faster and faster until he finished squirting.

Once she hung up the phone, Myah thought for a second about their conversation, and could have sworn that Irk was trying to rush her off, but she let it go since she had things she had to do, like get something to eat. The only reason she called Irk was because she felt guilty about busting a nut without him. Now that she was free this weekend, she had no worries and could enjoy herself.

Henry cleaned himself up, changed his khaki pants and went out to the yard with a smile on his face. Not only was he getting out in a couple of weeks, but he was also going to have a fine ass young bitch be his first piece of pussy after being down for twelve years straight. Yeah, Luscious had jerked him off a couple of times when she came to visit, but that wasn't the same as sliding his dick into some soft, hot, wet, young tight pussy.

As he walked over towards the basketball courts to kick it with some of his homies, his mind constantly went back to Myah. There was something about her that kept bugging his conscience. He always thought to himself whenever he saw her pictures or saw her in person that he had seen her someplace before. But being how old she was, it was literally impossible. He's been locked up for twelve years, and knowing that she was only eighteen years old would have made her six years old when he got knocked.

He continuously tried to shake the thought away, but no matter how many times he did, they kept coming back. "Too many drugs," he said out loud as he crossed over the patch of grass that separated the basketball courts from the handball courts.

His boy, Big Swope was trying his best to imitate Charles Barklay as he drove to the hoop, scoring a point for his team. They were playing a full court game of five-on-five.

"Eight-three!" one of the guys said before passing the ball to his guard.

"Nah, it's seven-four. Mike just scored on Jimmy before that," another guy said from the opposing team.

After they settled the score, both teams continued to play.

When there was a break in the game, Big Swope acknowledged Henry with a nod of his head. Everyone that was sitting on the benches watching either gave him dap or shook there heads as if to say, "What's up?"

Henry took a seat next to his homie, Bear who was smoking a Newport. "Let me hit that, big homie," Henry asked after getting settled on the bench.

Bear passed him the rest of his cigarette and continued to watch the game.

After Henry finished smoking, he threw it on the ground, looked over at Bear, who was now talking to the guy next to him, and waited for him to finish. Once he did, Henry asked him, "So, who you rooting for?"

"Ah shit! My big man, Swope! His team has been out there since rec move, beating the shit outta these niggas," Bear answered excitedly.

Henry, Bear and Swope hung out together most of the time. You rarely saw one without the other, but since Swope's time was almost up, he had been trying to get his priorities in order, so he didn't hang out much any more. Bear had some more years to do, so Henry decided not to mention the parole thing to him just yet, until they were back in the units.

"Yo, when we get back inside, I need to holla at'cha for a second, a'ight?" Henry said without looking in Bear's direction.

"What's wrong, Hen-Dog? You gotta problem with one of these niggas or something?"

Henry knew that Bear was a loose cannon and would go at the drop of a dime. That was one of the reasons why he fucked with him. The other was because Bear was good peoples. He would give his last to a homie if he needed it. Everyone respected him in the joint, but everyone also knew that he had a gang of time to do, and would probably never see the streets again. That's why Henry promised to look out for his man once he touched the bricks. "Nah, it's nothing like that. Damn! A nigga just can't kick it with his homie once in a while?" Henry asked jokingly.

Bear looked at him in the eyes and saw that Henry wasn't serious, and smiled. "My bad! My bad! You have to realize where we're at, and you'll understand why I asked that question."

Henry knew exactly what he was saying, and felt bad for bringing it up. No more was said about it as both men finished watching the rest of the game until the bell rang for yard recall.

When they got back to the unit, Henry told Bear about his parole being granted, which would let him out a year earlier. And while Bear acted happy about the news, Henry knew that he was hurting on the inside. Not only was Bear losing Big Swope in a couple of months, but now he was about to lose Henry as well. Henry assured him that he would be well taken care of, since he considered Bear like family. Ever since Henry had arrived at Danamora, Bear had treated him well, and he was going to do the same for him.

The next thing Henry had to do was start preparing for his release. Before he had to lockdown for the evening, he made a call to Luscious. He informed her of the good news and told her about his plan. She was to make sure things were set up for him before he touched the bricks.

Luscious loved Henry and would do just about anything he wanted her to do. So when he called, she jumped at the chance to please him. In her mind, Henry was her man, especially after all the time she had put in, and not to mention the loyalty she's shown throughout his bid. Her job was to make sure he had a place to stay in order for his parole officer to inspect it. Luscious just knew that she and Henry would be together eventually once everything was squared away. But, Henry had other ideas.

Henry told himself after he hung up with Luscious, that he had to sign up for the required pre-release classes, which consisted of learning how to write résumés for potential jobs, how to prepare for life on the outside by taking different life-skills classes, and how to manage the money he would make once he did get a job. He wasn't concerned about any of that.

What he was concerned about was the burning desire to get even with his late son's mother, Libretta—Libra for short. As he sat on his bunk bed and re-read the last letter that she wrote to him, the only thing he could think about was what he was going to do to her after what she put him and his son through. Revenge was heavy on his mind as he fell asleep for the night, clutching a picture of his son in his right hand.

TEN

"Damn, Nikki! We can't do this anymore!" Myah said as she rolled over on Nikki's twin bed.

"Myah, you say that every time you finish cumming! You would think that after — how many times have we done this? Oh yeah — a lot — you would have stopped saying that by now!" Nikki grabbed the towel that she had close by the bed and wiped her face of Myah's pussy juice.

They were both naked in the bed with the lights on, shades drawn shut, and the door locked so that no one would be able to see what they were doing. After what Keisha had done to them back in high school, they weren't about to let it happen again.

Myah rolled over to face Nikki, who was about to get out of bed to grab her clothes, and said, "I know I say that every time, and I do mean it, but it seems that you have a way of convincing me to do otherwise."

"Don't even say that. You know damn well that it takes two to tango, so don't put it off on me, making it sound as if I twisted your arm or something!" Nikki got up, walked over to her closet, and picked out something to put on for the evening. They were going to BackStreets, a club downtown in Potsdam where all of the underage students went to party the night away.

It was ten-forty p.m., and as usual, the club doesn't start jumping until midnight, so Nikki had plenty of time to jump in the shower and get dressed.

"I know, I know! But it just feels funny afterwards," Myah confessed while she stretched out her thick frame.

Nikki glanced at her beautiful black figure against her satin sheets, and thought about going at it again, but decided not to push her luck. It was always a struggle to get her to agree to letting her eat her pussy, so instead, Nikki turned away and looked back inside her closet.

What led up to this, Myah thought, was that the football game they went to earlier that day really wasn't as exciting as they thought it would be. It was cold, crowded, and on top of that, the team that they were rooting for lost 56-17. On the way back to Nikki's dorm, they had grabbed a bite to eat at one of the little shops that was located off the St. Lawrence University campus.

Once they ate, Myah wanted to take a shower and rest before they headed out for the night. She was staying at Nikki's for the weekend, since it didn't make any sense for her to keep driving back and forth between the two schools.

While she was drying off from the shower in Nikki's full-length mirror, Nikki walked in with a small towel wrapped around her head, and a larger one wrapped around her small frame.

Myah's shocked expression made Nikki laugh. "What's wrong with you?" she asked as she walked over to her bed and sat down to dry her hair.

Myah turned around to face her and caught Nikki staring at her lower region where Myah only had on a pair of apple green lace thongs. "Nikki! Stop looking at me like that! You know you make me feel uncomfortable when you do that!" Myah turned back around to look in the mirror at herself, but instead, she saw Nikki getting up and walking towards her. Myah tensed up, not knowing what to expect. Even though she knew she was into men and loved dick, she couldn't stop her mind from wandering, especially whenever she was around Nikki. Nikki was the only one that she had ever had a lesbian experience with.

After that night in her apartment, the only thing Myah could think about was how hard she had cum with Nikki licking her pussy. She was like a crack head that had their first hit of crack, and was hooked. Now, each time they took a hit, they were always chasing the feeling that they had the first time.

Nikki placed her hand on Myah's waist, put her face next to hers, and pressed her body up against Myah's and whispered in her ear, "You know you need to release all of that built-up tension you have, don't you?"

The way that Nikki spoke in her ear gave Myah goose bumps. Her body started to feel hot, and she was beginning to get wet. She moved away from Nikki's embrace, gathered herself and said, "Not today, Nikki. We need to stop this. I love dick, and you don't have one."

"But I have a tongue that knows how to please you like one," Nikki stated as she playfully stuck her tongue out and moved it around seductively, letting Myah know that she was willing to do whatever it took to get between her thick ass thighs.

Myah tried to put up a verbal fight, but it fell on deaf ears, as Nikki was determined to have her way. Even though Myah was physically stronger than she was, Nikki's aggressiveness always won out in the end.

"Look. After you get off one time, you'll feel better. I promise," Nikki added, trying to convince Myah to give in.

"That's what you always say, then it goes on and on and on. It's like you can't get enough!"

"I can't help it that your pussy's so sweet. I'm helpless when I'm down there, licking up all that sweet nectar," Nikki explained shyly.

It went back and forth, until finally Myah's body gave in to her desires. Her pussy was throbbing, and she did need a good nut. "A'ight! A'ight! Only one. After that, you gotta stop, okay?"

Nikki smiled, then let her towel fall to the floor, leaving her fully exposed. Myah turned her head, walked to the bed and laid down, slipping her thongs to the floor. *That was three hours ago,* Myah thought to herself as she watched Nikki get ready.

"You'd better get dressed if you want to get there before it gets packed" Nikki stressed while applying cherry flavored lip-gloss to her lips.

As Nikki was getting herself ready in the mirror, Myah laid in the bed and thought about the life that she was leading. She had a good man back at home who was a major drug kingpin, and a best friend that she was having a secret affair with. And to top it all off, she was tricking a man into believing that she was interested in him, when in fact, she was plotting to kill him for murdering her mother thirteen years ago. "What a life!" she said out loud as she sat up in the bed.

"What did you say?" Nikki asked once she saw the smirk on Myah's face.

"Nothing. I was just thinking about something, that's all."

"Well, do you care to share it?"

Myah looked at Nikki, who was now standing up in front of the mirror, adjusting the black leather Armani Exchange belt that she put around her small waist to accessorize her outfit. "Not really," she managed to say as she got out of the bed, butt ass naked, and walked over to the chair that held her jeans and sweater.

"Let me find out!" Nikki replied.

Myah noticed that Nikki was using that phrase a lot lately, which really didn't make any sense to her. "Let you find out what?"

"That you were thinking about me between those thick thighs of yours."

Myah had three orgasms, which left her a little drained. After hearing what Nikki had just said, she quickly got dressed and sat down in the chair to put on her boots. "No! Don't flatter yourself, Ms. Lick-a-lot!"

They both laughed, and then got themselves ready for the evening in silence.

While Myah and Nikki were just entering Club BackStreets, Tony was backstage at a concert that Tha PotHeadz were headlining. The crowd was chanting the chorus of one of the songs that the group was about to perform:

> *"...Niggas real to this, Sol-dier.*
> *Niggas die for this, yeah-h-h-h.*
> *Niggas ride for this, you don't kno-o-ow,*
> *Fucking' with them fugitives..."*

Just before Jerico was about to rip his sixteen bars, Tony's cell phone started ringing. He fumbled in his inside pocket of his black leather jacket and retrieved his Motorola, which indicated that the call was long distance.

"Yeah, what's up?" he yelled into the receiver while his right hand covered his ear so that he could hear whomever clearly. The crowd was hyped, which made it difficult to hear, but he managed as he moved away from the stage. "Who's this?"

While Tony tried to hear who it was that was calling him, one of the stagehands came over to him and whispered in his other ear, "Someone wants to see you. You might want to see this person, if you know what I mean!" the tall black young man said before he turned to walk away.

Tony looked in the direction that the stagehand was heading, and saw Kevin Lowe, the president of Streetlife Records, standing off to the side with his entourage, looking in his direction. "Yo! Whoever this is, call me back later!" Tony quickly said as he flipped his phone shut, cutting off whoever it was, and followed the stagehand towards the man that was responsible for his group's future.

"The club's jumpin' tonight! Look at how packed it is, and it's only twelve-thirty!" Nikki screamed in Myah's ear as they walked towards the dance floor. They had just entered the club after only ten minutes in line. One of Nikki's friends saw her and Myah waiting, and slipped the bouncer a ten to get them in, which made those in line ahead of them start cussing at the bouncer.

After spending some time with the guy that got them in, they headed to the bar to get themselves something to drink. Once they did, they made their way towards the dance floor, where young kids were provocatively dancing to Gwen Stefani's new song, featuring Eve.

The music was so loud that Myah couldn't hear what

Nikki was saying. "Huh?"

Nikki kept it moving, making her way towards an empty table that was situated off to the side of the dance floor, away from the rowdy crowd, so that they could sit and sip their drinks in peace.

While making their way over to the table, a couple of guys spotted them passing by and commented to each other. "Damn! Look at shorty over there with the burgundy sweatpants on!" Darrel said excitedly.

"Where?" his boy, Jay Dub asked, trying to find who Darrell was talking about. There were so many fine ass girls up in there that it was hard to pinpoint or single out just one.

"Look, over there!" Darrell stated as he pointed at Myah and Nikki

"Da-a-a-amn!" Jay Dub said once he saw Myah's ass in her DKNY burgundy velour sweatpants. He wasn't the only one looking at the girls as they sat down at the empty table. There were about five other guys scoping them out as well, trying to get up the courage to go and holla at the two lovelies.

Myah and Nikki were unaware of the attention that they were receiving, until Myah looked around the club and saw all eyes on her. Guys were dancing with their girls, but looking in their direction. She spotted a few others off to the side just staring at them, as if she was the main event. Before she could say anything about it to Nikki, she heard a male's voice behind her say, "Hey, ladies. What's poppin' for the evening?"

Myah turned around and recognized the guy from one of her classes she had on Wednesdays. Without saying a word, she turned back around to face the dance floor, ignoring the young man's attempt at macking.

Nikki, who didn't know any better, encouraged him

in conversation, until Myah kicked her leg under the table, as if to say, "What are you doing, bitch?"

"Ouch!" Nikki quietly screamed, causing the guy to look puzzled as to why she would react like that. The club was dark, since the lights were dimmed.

The music coming from the speakers that were situated throughout the small club was loud, and people were moving about aimlessly, either trying to get their drinks on, or trying to catch anyone that would give them some play.

"Excuse me, but my friend and I are trying to relax *alone*. Thank you!" Myah turned and said to the young guy in a sarcastic tone of voice.

The guy, who was hip to rejection, played it off, then stepped, leaving Myah and Nikki alone as they wished.

Once he was out of earshot, Myah leaned over towards Nikki and said, "Are you crazy?"

Nikki rubbed her leg a few times, then responded, "You didn't have to kick my leg like that. Shit hurts like a muthafucker!"

"Well, that was the only way I could get your attention, Ms. Easy Pickings!"

"Excuse me! I'm sorry if guys are more attracted to the white meat than the dark!" Nikki shot back, trying to be funny.

Myah didn't like what she said. She then went about proving to her friend that she could get anyone in the club that she wanted, if she so desired. "Oh yeah? Well, we'll see what guys go for, if that's what you wanna do!"

"Fine!"

Myah got up, straightened out her sweatpants, then walked over towards a group of guys that were standing against the back wall, and started dancing to the music right in front of them, which got their attentions quick.

Nikki watched as one of the guys came up behind Myah and rubbed his groin up against her ass, trying to keep in step with what she was doing. Myah, instead of stopping him, pushed her ass into him and looked up at Nikki, who was becoming more and more jealous by the minute. Myah knew that Nikki would be mad, but she didn't care. The guy behind her was becoming more bold as his friends chanted him on, which caused the crowd to stop and stare at what Myah and her dance partner were doing.

Nikki got her drink, walked over to the dance floor, and watched jealously as Myah danced provocatively with the tall black guy, who was grabbing her hips in order to keep up with her. They looked as if they were fucking doggy style by the way Myah was bend over, and the guy was pushing himself up against her.

The song changed just as Myah turned around to face her dance partner. She wrapped her arms around his neck and moved in closer, rubbing her chest up against his, and coming within inches of his face. The young guy's friends were floored at how Myah was acting, and the guy himself couldn't believe his luck. They moved together to the music without one of them saying a word, until someone in the crowd grabbed her ass.

Myah quickly turned around to see who did it, and was surprised to see another tall guy smiling at her, with the sexiest hazel green eyes she had ever seen on a light skinned brother.

"My bad, shorty! I thought you were someone else."

Myah let go of her dance partner, walked up to him, looked up into his eyes and said, "I could be who you're looking for!"

The brother was stunned by her response, and wasn't prepared for it at all. He knew that she wasn't any one he knew, and only did it to impress his friends. What he thought was going to happen didn't, and now he was left speechless as Myah moved closer to him in order to admire his eyes. Nikki had had enough. She walked over to Myah, grabbed her arm and pulled her back over towards their table. The whole time, Myah was looking at the tall brother with the hazel green eyes.

The guy that was dancing with her first was pissed off that his dance had ended early. He waited until the light skinned brother turned back around from clocking Myah's ass to check him. "Hey, homie, that was some sucker shit you did!"

The light skinned brother didn't say a word, but quickly reacted with a right hand punch to the tall guy's jaw, causing the dance floor to erupt into a free-for-all.

The light skinned guy's friends threw down their drinks and went about beating whomever thought about jumping in.

Security reacted quickly, and the fight was broken up. The bouncers threw both guys out of the club, along with their homies, leaving everyone that was left inside in a state of shock.

Once everyone was straight, one of the bouncers gave a thumbs-up to the DJ to continue the music, which he responded with a head nod and put on Master P's single, "Make You Say Unnn".

Myah couldn't believe what had just happened, but smiled at Nikki and said, "See! I'm still *that* bitch that can make niggas fight for all of this!" She slapped her ass, indicating that they were fighting over her body.

Nikki, who still looked shaken, turned towards Myah and said, "Let's get out of here." She started walking towards the exit, with Myah two steps behind her.

ELEVEN

Sunday morning, Myah woke up with a smile on her face. She stretched out her body, then realized that Nikki was still asleep. They kept the beds together the whole weekend, and slept side by side. Last night was exhausting. After the club, they returned to Nikki's dorm, where they drank a little more, then fooled around until they both fell asleep.

Now, as Myah thought back to what had happened at the club, she giggled to herself, then climbed slowly out of bed so as not to wake up her sleeping friend. She found Nikki's slippers next to the bed and put them on so that she could go to down the hallway to the bathroom to brush her teeth. Before opening the door, she put on her sweatpants and one of Nikki's long white T-shirts that had the school's name across the chest. Her bra and panties were somewhere near the bed, which she didn't feel like looking for. It was eight twenty-three, still too early to be up, but she knew she had a lot to do today. She planned on keeping her word to go visit Hendrick that afternoon.

While in the bathroom, she looked at herself in the mirror and saw that her hair was a mess. Before she had a chance to straighten it out with her fingers, a heavy-set white girl came through the bathroom door wearing a pair of tight shorts that appeared to be lost in the many rolls in her legs, and a tank top that would have looked good on anybody else but her.

"Oh, good morning. I didn't know anyone was in here," the overweight girl said after seeing Myah at the sink.

Myah noticed that she wasn't wearing any shoes of any kind, which, in itself, was nasty, considering that the bathroom floor was damp and dirty. "Hey, what's up?" she quickly responded, trying to avoid eye contact with the wildebeast.

The young girl walked over to one of the stalls, opened the door, squeezed her large frame inside, then sat down on the toilet to take a piss, the whole time leaving the stall door open for anyone to see. Myah, who was looking in the mirror at the girl, frowned her face and looked down, not wanting to see any more of the disgusting white trash's behavior. She tried to finish what she was doing in order to leave, but the white girl continued to converse with her.

"Weren't you down at BackStreets last night with Nikki?"

"Yeah. Why? What's up?"

The white girl flushed the toilet and waited for the noise to subside before continuing. "Oh, I was just asking. That was some fight they had down there. Damn! They were fighting over you, right?" she asked, already knowing the answer.

Myah thought about the question, turned around to face the big girl, who was now coming out of the stall, and said, "What makes you say that?"

"'Cause after you left, I heard that boy with the light green eyes say to one of his friends that no one was going to fuck with you as long as he was around."

Myah must have looked confused, because the girl also added, "Yeah, then he got into a Jeep Cherokee and followed Nikki's car. You didn't know him?"

"Hell no!" Myah answered, wondering what the hell that was all about.

The girl came over to the sink to wash her hands, causing Myah to move over in order to give her some room.

"Well, he sure acted like he knew you. He was fine as hell too!" she said with a smirk on her face.

Myah dismissed it all, said she had to go, and walked out of the bathroom. Once she was back in the room, she saw Nikki was sitting up in bed, drinking a bottle of water that she had left next to the bed last night.

"There you go! I thought you just left without saying good-bye, until I saw your panties on the floor," Nikki said, holding up Myah's apple green thongs with one finger and smiling devilishly.

Myah placed her toothbrush and toothpaste in her carry bag, walked over to the bed and grabbed her panties from off of Nikki's finger before she had a chance to sniff them, as she was threatening to do. "Thank you for finding them for me," Myah stated as she sat on the bed to put them on.

"So, what do you have planned for today?"

"Well, I have to go up to Clinton to visit my friend this afternoon, then I'm—"

Myah didn't get a chance to finish before Nikki interrupted her. "Myah, when is this going to stop? It was cute back in high school, but damn! It's not like you're going to be with him or anything like that, right?"

Myah smiled, and thought about the real reason she was still doing what she was doing. She got up, put on her clothes, and walked over towards the mirror. "My-a-a-ah! What do you see in him any way? He's a criminal that's probably lying to you about when he's getting out. You remember what Jennifer went through with that guy from prison about a year ago, don't you?"

Myah knew that Nikki didn't know the real reason for her interest in Hendrick, and she wasn't about to tell her now. She just let Nikki think what she wanted to think.

"Besides, you don't need another dick in your life! It's bad enough you're still fucking around with that drug lord, Irk, which I still don't see why you're still with him. He's old enough to be your father. You know he's out there fucking God knows who!"

Myah had heard enough and put her hand up to say so. "Nikki, what's wrong with you? You sound as if you're my man or something! Let it go, girlfriend. Seriously. I know what I'm doing. You're acting like one of these guys out here that's trying to control a bitch after getting a piece of pussy."

Nikki looked shocked at what Myah had just said. "Well, I'm sorry for caring about a bitch! I was just—"

"You were just what, Nik?' Trying to protect me? Please! What you were doing was sounding like you were a jealous boyfriend."

"But Myah, you don't *need* anyone but me! I could take care of you. Damn, it's not like I don't have plenty of fucking money to do so!"

They stood at opposite ends of the room, just staring at one another, until Myah finally walked over towards Nikki's closet to grab her duffel bag and jacket. Nikki quickly moved towards her to stop her, but Myah was already opening the door to leave.

"Myah, wait! You can't just leave like this. All I wanted to do was to help you realize that nobody's going to love you like I will!"

Not wanting to cause a scene in Nikki's hallway, Myah stepped back inside, closed the door, then in a quiet voice said, "Nikki, I know you love me, and I do understand that you don't want to see me hurt. But for you to act like you are is really scaring me. You hurt my feelings once you brought the money factor in. You make it sound as if I'm some gold digging bitch or something. You know me better than that, so for you to say that, yeah, it hurt me."

Myah turned back around to leave, until Nikki screamed, "I'm sorry!" The tears in her eyes made Myah turn back to comfort her best friend.

At eleven forty-eight, Henry was getting himself prepared for what he hoped was a visit from Myah. She had told him that on Sunday she would be there, and usually she was very good at keeping her word. He knew that if she was coming to visit, she would be there between twelve and one o'clock.

Their last visit didn't go so well, so he wanted to make sure she knew that he was sorry for the way he reacted, and for disrespecting her by even asking her to do something so dumb. Besides, if he was going to tap that young phat ass of hers, he knew that he had to keep her happy, especially since he planned on telling her of his early release once they were situated in their seats.

"Damn, girl! Where the fuck are you?" he questioned as he looked at his Timex watch that he bought from the commissary in Elmira. He knew that the chances of her coming to visit were fifty-fifty, but he hoped for the best and prepared for the worst. "Failing to prepare is preparing to fail," is what his man from Brooklyn used to say to him whenever he would have a basketball game. While he stretched out on his bunk to rest a little, he thought about the streets and what he should expect once he got out. A lot of things have changed since he's been away, but hustling would never change, and he knew how to do that very well. Henry figured he would have to round up about four or five good guys to work with, and he would be back on top within a few months. That's what he was thinking before a male correctional officer came to his door to inform him that his visitor was there.

"Anderson, visit!" the officer yelled into his cell, startling him out of his thoughts.

Henry jumped up, put on his white pair of low-cut Airforce Ones, leaving the laces undone, looked in the mirror one last time to make sure everything looked good, then stepped out of his cell and headed towards the officers' station.

Myah waited in line for about fifteen minutes before she was admitted inside of the visitors' section of the building. A female guard directed her into a room that was no bigger than a coat closet in order to pat search her before allowing her to enter the visiting room.

"Do you have anything that would be considered contraband?" the pretty middle aged black woman asked before physically searching Myah.

"No!"

"Alright. Please turn around and face the wall," she commanded. She waited until Myah was spread against the wall, then proceeded to pat her down, starting with her chest, and going down each leg. The officer knew that the inmates would have young girls such as Myah mule drugs in for them, so she paid special attention when searching them.

To Myah, it was sort of ridiculous, considering the fact that each visitor had to pass through a series of metal detectors before getting to this point, but then again, this was a maximum facility that took security seriously.

After the guard was satisfied that Myah was clean, she handed her the clear purse that contained a roll of quarters, a pack of gum, and some napkins.

Myah walked through the door, found two empty chairs, sat down and waited for Hendrick to be called.

It was twelve thirty-four, Myah noted. "Only twenty minutes this time," she said to herself as she mentally calculated how long it usually took her to get to this point. Even though she'd been here a few times before, it always amazed her when she looked around and saw the bars over the windows and all of the fine men that were locked away in this hell hole they called a prison. The place always freaked her out whenever she came up. From the look of the building from the outside, to how it looked on the inside, it wasn't what she expected it to be.

While she was thinking about how the place looked, Henry came through the back door, placed his ID card in the slot near the officer's desk, and looked around before spotting Myah in the back where they usually sat whenever she came to visit. Even though it was early, the visiting room was still a little crowded with young girls and their kids visiting their baby daddies, to mothers or wives visiting their sons or husbands. One thing was for sure; all of the younger girls wore tight fitting clothes that left nothing to the imagination. The tighter, the better, and

Myah was no exception.

Myah was wearing a short sleeved, see-through baby blue blouse that covered her black lace Victoria's Secret bra, and a pair of white Parasuco Capri pants with a baby blue leather belt that matched her blouse. On her feet were a pair of baby blue and white Nike AirMax sneakers, with no socks. The Capri pants were so tight on her that some of the guards and even other inmates took notice of her voluptuous body when she stood up to greet Henry with a hug and a kiss.

"Hey, baby!" Myah said excitedly, mostly for his pleasure, while on the inside, she was a little repulsed and didn't want to be there with him.

They sat down in their chairs, side by side, and Henry placed his arm around Myah's neck. "Damn! You're looking to good to be up in here," he said as he looked at her from head to toe. Myah's hair was pressed and lying to the right side of her face, her makeup, the little that she had on, was applied evenly to blend in with her natural complexion.

Henry looked at her thighs, and got instantly excited. He placed his left hand on her right thigh and rubbed up and down, feeling the contours of her muscular leg. She had her legs crossed, which made it harder for him to go any further than the top of her leg. "Daddy can't touch the merchandise, baby girl?" he whispered in her ear as he continued to rub her thigh slowly.

Myah uncrossed her legs for him, and replied, "You know you can, daddy."

His warm hand was causing her to get aroused, which was evident by the way her nipples were poking through her lace bra and blouse. "You better stop before they say something to us."

"Don't worry, they're not even paying us any attention."

After getting his little feels in, Henry decided to share the good news with her. "Hey, I have something to tell ya."

Myah looked into his eyes and realized that whatever it was that he wanted to tell her was obviously good news.

"They granted me early parole! I'll be out within the next two weeks!" He was smiling as he told her this, but Myah had a look of shock on her face, as if someone had just scared the shit out of her.

"That's, ummm, that's great, baby!" she replied, giving him a tight hug.

Henry hugged her back and placed his face in her hair and smelled apples. "Wow! Your hair smells real good. I can't wait to smell the rest of you once we're finally together!"

Myah's mind was racing with a thousand thoughts as she took it all in.

On the way back to her dorm, she left the music off and thought about everything that Henry had told her. All she could think about was him saying, "They granted me early parole!"

Winter, '01

Payback's
A
Bitch!

TWELVE

The mid-size office on the second floor of the 43rd Precinct was crowded with three large individuals, both in size and status. Detective Williamson was seated behind his desk, reading a Fax that he had received two days ago, which was the reason for retired Detective Moody and Detective Stevens' presence.

"Gentlemen, the reason why I've called you in today was to first of all, get your input on this situation, since you were also victims of Mr. Anderson's drug induced rage. And secondly, to draw your attention to certain things that I have found out concerning the connection between Sonya Johnson's unsolved murder thirteen years ago, and what I've now learned about her daughter, Myah Johnson," Williamson stated, hoping that he could get some help with what he planned on doing, unofficially.

Since there weren't any suspects in the murder of Sonya Johnson, the case had turned cold, and was left as unsolved. But from what Detectives Moody and Stevens were saying, there was plenty of circumstantial evidence that could have tied Hendrick Anderson to her murder. Now that his parole was granted, Detectives Moody and

Stevens were sent notification of his release date, along with a copy of the parole papers, as was the actual victim of the crime, Libretta Nichols, who was the reason for Anderson going to prison in the first place. Her safety was first and foremost, but they also knew that if they were to solve the murder of Sonya Johnson, they would have to use her daughter, Myah to draw him out.

"Well, since I'm retired now, it'll be sort of difficult for me to open up a can of worms that no one wants to touch anyway," Moody stated as he sat in one of the folding chairs that he and Stevens were given by Williamson.

"Yeah, I agree with that also," Stevens followed. They were both off of the force and enjoying their lives at home with their families now, but once they received their notifications from the Victim's Advocate Services, they contacted each other, then received a call from Detective Williamson for them to come in for a meeting with him today.

"As I understand it, you both have strong feelings that this is the guy responsible for that girl's murder, am I right?"

Both detectives nodded their heads in agreement, then leaned back in order to listen to the rest of what Detective Williamson had to say.

Libra, who was living in the Flatbush section of Brooklyn, was sitting on her bed, holding a letter that she received just yesterday from the Victim's Advocate Services of New York. Inside was a single piece of paper informing her of Henry's early release from prison. Her body tensed up as she opened up the envelope to read what it said:

Dear Ms. Nichols;

This notice is to inform you of the early release of Mr. H. Anderson. Parole had been granted to the above-named individual, due to the overcrowding of the New York State's prison system.

It is our duty to inform you of such, and to give you an opportunity to be prepared for this individual's release so that you can take the necessary precautions.

Mr. Anderson has been issued a Restraining Order to stay five hundred feet away from you at all times. If he violates the terms of this agreement, his parole will be revoked, and he will be sent back to prison to finish the remainder of his sentence.

If you have any questions or concerns, please feel free to contact (718) 555-4242 (Ext. 33).

Sincerely,
Mr. A.L. St. Range
Victim's Advocate Services of New York

Libra's eyes began to tear up as she thought about Henry being back on the streets. She knew that he would stay true to his word and get even with her for what she put him through, and for the death of Henry Jr. He blamed his death on her, and that alone made her scared out of her mind.

"How could they? How could they let him back on the streets after all these years?" she screamed as she crumpled the letter up into a ball and threw it on the floor. "I'm dead! I know it! He's gonna get me, I just know it!"

Every time he was up for parole, she would go to the Board and plead for them to deny him, which had worked for years. But, she didn't know about this one. She knew he would get out eventually, but she wasn't prepared for it to be this soon.

She got up from the bed, picked up the cordless phone and proceeded to dial. The phone was answered on the fourth ring. "Hello!" she said once she heard a woman's voice answer.

"May I help you?"

"Yes, you can. I need to speak with Derrick Jones, please. It's an emergency."

"Just a moment," the young woman replied as she went to get him from his work station in the back of the factory in which he worked.

After what seemed like forever, Derrick finally came on the line. "Yeah, what's up?"

Libra could hear the irritation in his voice, but she was too scared to even care. "Derrick, he's getting out!"

"Who tha fuck are you talking about?" he demanded.

"Henry, that's who!"

Derrick thought about the name, then once it registered, he quickly went into his "I don't give a fuck" attitude. "What tha fuck that's gotta do with me?"

"He thinks that we killed Henry Jr., and I know he's gonna try to do something stupid. What we gonna do?" Libra asked while tears welled up in her eyes.

Derrick didn't know what she was talking about, since he didn't have anything to do with her son's death. He wasn't even in town when all that went down. "What do you mean he thinks that we killed his son? I wasn't anywhere near him when he got hit by that truck. You're the one that wasn't watching his ass, since you wanted to fuck with that Herb ass nigga from 157th and Amsterdam.

Besides, why would he think that I had something to do
with that?"

Libra thought about telling him about the letter she
wrote to Henry, about Derrick letting Henry Jr. eat some
coke that they left on the table. Then she realized that it
would only make it worse, so she played it off by changing
the subject. "He knows that we were together, so he thinks
that you are as responsible as me. What we gonna do? You
know he's crazier than a muthafucka!"

Derrick listened to what she was saying, then
realized that they were docking him for the time he spent
on the phone. Even though he knew that he could care less
about this shitty ass job, he needed it in order to keep his
probation officer off his back. He was still getting his paper
selling coke, but he had to act as if he was rehabilitated
now. He wasn't trying to go back to Riker's again. "Hey, I
have to get back before they fire my black ass. Holla at me
when I get home tonight, you heard?" he said, not waiting
for her response. He hung up before she could tell him
that she was leaving town as soon as possible.

That night, Libra packed her bags with what she
could carry, and headed to the bus station to go to her
sister's house in New Jersey. She knew that she would be
safe there, since Henry didn't know where her sister lived.

Little did she know, her sister had been writing to
Henry about Henry Jr. before he died, and gave him her
address to write back. With that unknown to Libra, she
was running from the smoke, right into the fire, of which
she wasn't going to make it out alive.

THIRTEEN

Henry completed all of the necessary classes that he needed in order to satisfy his parole conditions, and now, the day had finally arrived for him to be released back into society.

"Mr. Anderson!" the bulky black male correctional officer yelled into Henry's cell in order to get his attention.

Henry was lying on his bunk, listening to his Walkman radio, waiting for someone to come and take him to the R&D Department.

"Anderson, let's go!"

Henry opened his eyes, took off his headphones and stood up to follow Officer Wilson. "Yeah, I'm outta here, mutha-fuckas!" he screamed to the other inmates in the dorm as he walked towards the door that led to the hallway.

"Yeah, my nigga! Be safe!" one guy yelled as he put his fist up to say peace.

"Don't forget about us little peoples, big homie!" another shouted from across the common area.

Henry nodded his head, then saw his boy, Karriem standing off to the side, smoking a cigarette. Henry walked over to him, gave him dap and a hug, and told him to take it easy. He wasn't going to forget what he did to make his stay in Danamora comfortable.

Last night, Henry hung out with his peoples, Bear and Big Swope one last time, and made sure he got all of their information in order to stay in touch. Big Swope was going home in a couple of months. He didn't need too much from him. But Bear, who was a lifer, was the main reason why Henry came to holler. He wanted Bear to know that he had him once he got his shit together, which Henry knew would be sooner than later. "Don't worry, Bear, I got you. That's my word! On everything I love, my nigga. You ain't gonna need for nothing!" Henry stated as he walked away to head back in for recall.

Now, it was nine o'clock on a Wednesday morning, and henry was walking towards the R&D building to pack out and go home. He was going to catch a bus back to the Bronx, but Luscious insisted on picking him up at the front gate.

As he slipped on the clothes that he had sent up a week ago, he thought about Myah and all of the shit that he was going to do to that pretty young thing once he got his hands on her. He couldn't wait to tap that fine ass of hers, but that would have to wait until he was situated. He wasn't worried. He knew that in time, it would come. He put on his peanut butter Tims and black leather jacket, then waited for the CO to give him his personal property so that he could be on his way.

"One Gucci leather wallet, a pair of sunglasses, a gold chain with religious medallion, and a check for fifteen hundred dollars," the receiving officer said as she handed Henry all of his things.

After putting all of his effects into his pocket, Henry was led to a side door and handed over to Officer Johnson,

an officer that wasn't favored by any of the inmates there —
Henry being one of them.

"Well, Mr. Anderson! Today is the day, huh?" Johnson
said with a smirk on his face as he walked Henry towards
the front gate to be released.

Henry didn't say a word, which caused Johnson to
get an attitude. "Anyway, you'll be back, or someone will
murda your black ass. One or the other, but I'm willing it
to be the other."

That statement made Henry furious, but he knew
that what Officer Johnson was doing was just trying to
provoke him into a confrontation, which would violate
his parole, and that wasn't going to happen. Henry just
stayed quiet until he reached the gate that led to the street
where Luscious was waiting for him in her Subaru Legacy.

Once Officer Johnson called for the gate to be opened,
Henry said in a low voice, "Hey, Johnson. You's a bitch
ass nigga, but you already know that. What you don't
know is that niggas have been pissing in your coffee cup
for months! And the funny thing about that is, I think
you actually liked it!" As the gate opened up fully, Henry
stepped away from Johnson, laughing at the look on his
face after what he had just told him.

"If that's true, Anderson, I hope your black ass do
come back here just so that I can torment you even more!"

Henry kept walking, not wanting to acknowledge
the statement that was just said. Once he was past the
gate's entrance, it started to close with him on one side,
and Officer Johnson on the other. Henry turned around
to face him, flipped him the finger and said, *"Fuck you!"*
in a loud voice, then turned back around, got in on the
passenger side of Luscious' car and drove off.

"But, I thought you would want some pussy, since you've been locked up for so many years now!" Luscious said after composing herself.

Henry did want a shot of pussy, just not from her. They were in his apartment after the eight-hour ride from Danamora. On the way to the Bronx, Luscious pulled over at the first rest stop they came to on the thruway, parked in a secluded spot away from those that came there to eat, use the restroom or to gas up, in order to give Henry some head. It took only three minutes for him to cum, which Luscious had expected. It was all part of her plan to get him to stay hard without cumming once they were able to be alone in his apartment. Now that they were, he didn't want to be with her. It made her feel undesirable, then used all in one.

"I got things I have to do before I can set my mind on some pussy," Henry replied after seeing the disappointed look on her face.

"I've been waiting for this day for a while, and all you can say is, 'I have things to do'? Nigga, please. Either you had some pussy while you were there, or your ass is gay! It ain't too many niggas gonna pass up on this!" she said as she pointed to her breasts and ass. "Especially coming out of prison."

Henry looked at her body as she stood in the doorway of his bedroom, stark as naked, and felt himself getting hard, but quickly tried to hide it, not wanting her to know he was feeling her like that.

She saw it growing inside of his jeans and commented on it. "Obviously someone wants to play with this!" she stated, pointing to her pussy.

Henry got up, walked over towards her, wrapped his arms around her waist, pulled her close to him and whispered in her right ear, "We have time. Just be patient. Let me take care of what I have to do. Then, I promise you this, you will get this and all you're looking for."

Luscious' pussy was getting wetter by the second as he touched her waist. His hand went down towards her thigh, and she spread her legs apart in anticipation of his caress towards her pussy lips. When he stopped just inches before it, she became irate. "Then stop teasing a bitch!" she said as she pulled away from his embrace and walked towards the bathroom to get the clothes that she had left on the floor.

She had taken a shower just minutes before, hoping that he would come in with her, but when he didn't, she came out, only to find that he was on the phone, talking to someone. She thought it was another girl, so she climbed into his bed with nothing on, hoping that the sight of her body would entice him to pay her some attention. But, when it didn't work, she laid next to him until he hung up so that she could give him a piece of her mind.

Once he was off the phone, Henry looked at Luscious, who was now rolling her eyes at him, and calmly said, "Bitch, get your shit and get the fuck outta here before I break my foot off in your fat ass!"

The look on her face was one of total shock. She couldn't believe what she had just heard. The words that came out of her mouth were twisted with anger, fear and bewilderment. "W-w-w-what!" was all that she could manage to say before Henry jumped out of bed and hovered over her in a threatening manner.

"You heard what tha fuck I said! I tried to be nice, but your ass is just pissing me off. Get your shit and get tha fuck on!"

Luscious quickly rolled out of bed, grabbed her clothes and shoes, went to the bathroom and got dressed. Henry heard the door lock and smiled to himself because he knew that she wasn't expecting him to act like that. He was pissed off at the fact that she had the audacity to question his authority and think that she was running shit.

He waited until she opened the door and came out with her face in tears before he decided to take her up on her offer. He knew that what he was about to do would confuse her, but he would be crazy to let her fine ass leave here without knocking her back out, which he intended to do from the beginning, but on his terms. "Come here!" he yelled as he sat down on his bed.

"What?"

"I said, come here!" Henry was enjoying the game that he was playing with her. It excited him, which was evident by the bulge in his jeans. The strain was just too much for him to bear, so as Luscious cautiously walked over towards him, he started to unbuckle his pants in order to free his dick, which was as hard as steel.

"Why are you playing with me-e-e-e?" Luscious asked between sobs.

Henry smiled at the way she was acting, and playfully answered, "'Cause you've been a bad girl! Now, let daddy get some of that candy."

Luscious walked between his legs, dropped down on her knees, took his hard dick into her hand and proceeded to give the best blowjob of his life. Her oral skills were the best that Henry had ever experienced, but it was the way that she contracted her pussy muscles that really drove him crazy.

After an hour of pounding her out, Henry was exhausted. They both were sweaty and spent, and as they laid in the bed panting, the phone rang, which caused

Henry to jump up. He grabbed the cordless from off of the nightstand next to him, and answered it on the third ring. "Yeah?"

"It's ready. Meet me in fifteen minutes at the spot I told you about earlier."

Henry smiled as he placed the phone back on the nightstand.

"Who's that, baby? Is everything a'ight?" Luscious asked in her softest voice, not wanting him to get out of bed.

"Yeah, everything's good. Where's your keys at?" I have to take care of something real quick." He hopped out of bed, put on his jeans and Timberlands, then found his gray hoodie, which was lying on the floor near the bathroom door, and slipped it on before he went in to the bathroom to take a piss.

Luscious sat up in bed, exposing her perky tits and yelled where he could find her keys. She contemplated whether she should ask him where he was going, or even if he would be back anytime soon, then thought better of it, not wanting what happened earlier to happen again.

The special moment that they shared was still fresh in her mind, not to mention the pain she was still experiencing from him beating her pussy up. It was all that she thought it would be. After sucking him off for the second time that day, he lasted longer than she expected. She tried everything to get him to cum early, but it was like he was the Energizer Bunny. He just kept on going, and going, and going… When he did finally bust his third nut, she managed to milk him dry with the technique she learned from reading that "Kama Sutra" book. Even though she was upset that he was leaving, her body was relieved that he was. She needed the rest. Plus, her poor kitty-kat needed to recuperate for what she knew would be round two once he came back. That thought alone brought a smile to her face as she laid back down, placing her head on the soft downy pillow she had bought for his king-size bed.

Big O was sitting in his triple black 2000 Escalade that was resting on shiny black twenty-inch Geovani rims. He was waiting for Henry to meet him in order to hand him the black leather bag that contained two kilos of Peruvian flake cocaine, and fifty thousand dollars in cash. When Henry called him, Big O was in the process of bagging up the last of his work before he was to recoup. He had told Henry to wait until he got back from his connect, so that he could bless him lovely for his first day of freedom.

They had met three years before while they were in Elmira State Penn. From that first day, they hit it off. And since Big O was going to be hitting the bricks first, he made a promise to Henry that once he touched down, he would bless him with a little something for what he had done for him while they were in the joint. Now that Henry was out, Big O intended to make good on his word.

As he waited with his man, Juicy, from Brooklyn, they saw a burgundy sedan creeping up slowly in his side view mirror. The block was quiet, which was one of the reasons why Big O had picked it to do the transaction. Once the car passed by allowing O to look inside, he recognized the driver and flashed his high beams three times for Henry to pull over. Before he called him back with the okay, he told Henry to creep slowly down the one way street, then stop at the corner and wait for a signal. Big O was a little more cautious about his dealings now more than ever, especially since he knew how niggas rolled on one another. He heard and saw firsthand while locked up how snitching was becoming the norm for a lot of the younger cats in the game. Plus, he wasn't trying to get popped by the Feds who were handing niggas like him death sentences.

Henry pulled over to the side, parked and got out of his car. When Big O saw that he was alone, he rolled down his window and motioned for him to come over. "Da-a-a-mn! This that shit you were talking about?" Henry asked as he admired the whip that Big O was pushing.

"Nah, my nigga, that was the Suburban. This was a gift from a good friend. Yo, hop in so we can holla," Big O replied as he pressed the button to unlock the doors.

Once Henry opened the door, he saw that the truck was laced with all kinds of electronics. The headrest, which contained a seven and a half-inch TV screen, was playing a movie that he recognized to be "Scarface". "Say hello to my little friend!" was what he heard coming from the speakers that were situated throughout the truck. It was as if he was inside of a movie theater. The windows were blacked out so that only the occupants could see out, and no one could see in.

Henry closed the door, and Big O introduced him to Juicy. "Ayo, this is my man, Juicy. He's my right hand," Big O said while starting up the truck.

"What's up, homie?" Henry greeted with a nod of his head.

As they pulled out of the spot that Big O was parked in, Henry noticed a small knapsack on the seat next to him. Big O looked in his rearview mirror and saw that Henry was eyeing the bag, and said, "That's you, big homie."

Henry picked it up and felt that it had some weight to it. He unzipped the bag and looked inside. When he saw the two bricks, he smiled. "Now, that's what I'm talkin' about!" he said excitedly. He pulled out one of the taped bricks, then saw what looked to be a wad of money wrapped in thick rubber bands.

"Yeah, homie, that's all you. You should be able to get on your feet with that. Plus, there's fifty thousand dollars at the bottom for some spending money. Once you get situated, holla at me so that you can re-up." Big O continued to drive around the block until he came back to the same spot that they were at previously.

Juicy, who was quiet throughout the ride, finally spoke up. "If you have any problems, give me a call." He then handed Henry a small cell phone. "My number is in the memory. Just press one, and send. It'll dial directly to my cell."

"Good looking out, homie. That's love."

Juicy knew that Henry had been away for a minute, so when he heard him using that old slang, he looked over at Big O and smiled.

The look wasn't missed by Henry, who questioned it. "What's wrong?"

Big O parked in the spot, turned off the engine and turned around to face his homie. "Yo, son, since you've been away, the young ones around here talk a little differently. I had to adjust myself. Once you're around a bit, you'll see what I'm talking about."

Henry looked at Juicy, who was now facing forward, and realized that Big O was right. It had been a minute since he's been around his peoples. Plus, staying up north in those hick towns had rubbed off on him.

"Do you have a crew to work with yet?" O asked.

Henry thought about some of his old crew, then figured that they haven't been in contact with him since he's been locked up. "Nah, but I have some people in mind that I met since I've been down. You remember Skinner, the Dread in B-block?"

"Yeah. What's he been up to?"

"Well, he got out about a year ago, and I got his info. I'll holla at him once I get settled. He was a thorough nigga in the joint."

Before Henry could finish his thought, Big O stated, "Yo, we ain't in the joint anymore, and these streets are real grimy now. Just be careful who you deal with, homie."

That statement alone made Henry think. Big O was right. Niggas do change once they get out, but he wasn't going to be one of them.

FOURTEEN

Two days had passed, and still not a word from Henry, or where he was. Myah knew that he didn't know where she stayed while in school, but nevertheless, she was still concerned about running into him.

She offered to pick him up from prison, but he declined, which Myah was relieved, to say the least. Her plans were to get him to confess what he did to her mother, then to act out her revenge. She wanted to have him set up to be killed, but the only problem was, she didn't have the stomach to use Irk like she had intended. She never planned on falling in love with him.

Now, as she lay in his bed waiting for him to finish in the shower, she thought about other options. "I could get him sent back to prison by giving that detective some information. Nah, that wouldn't work. Aha! I could... nah... fuck! This is harder than I thought!" Myah said to herself.

"What's that, princess?" Irk asked as he walked into the bedroom with a towel wrapped around his waist.

Myah was taken aback a little. She never heard the shower stop, and when he spoke, it caught her totally off guard. "Ummm, nothing. I was just thinking about a paper I have to do for one of my professors this semester." Irk took the towel from around his waist, stood in front of his full-length mirror and dried himself off with it as Myah watched him from behind. She cleared her throat to get his attention, then once she did, she patted the space next to her for him to come to bed. The sight of his body brought a rush of sensations to her body. Her nipples started to get hard, and between her legs started to get moist. She spread her legs apart, then placed her hand between them. After getting her fingers wet, she pulled them out and stuck them in the air for Irk to see. "See what you're doing to me? I need a little sumptin' sumptin'," she exclaimed playfully.

Irk walked towards the bed with his dick in his hand, stroking it as he walked. Since his body was chiseled from the workouts he did at the gym, he had an air of confidence about him that Myah loved.

She was about to put her hand back between her legs, when Irk demanded that she don't. "No! Don't you dare! Give me your hand," he commanded in a stern voice.

Myah looked at him to see whether he was serious or joking, but before she could decide, he was on the bed with the same fingers that she had just stuck into her pussy inside his warm, moist mouth. He sucked and licked her fingers clean of any pussy juice that she had on them. After he was finished, he said in a soft voice, "Ummm, that was goo-o-o-od! I swear your shit tastes like candy!"

He leaned over her body and placed his lips on hers, and she too tasted herself on his tongue as they continued to kiss passionately. During their embrace, Irk managed to slip his fingers into her wet pussy lips, which caused her to gasp out loud. "Ahhhh!" He stopped kissing her lips, then moved to her neck, kissing his way down until he reached her ample breasts. Her nipples were erect, so he took one into his mouth and sucked on it for a minute. Then, he moved to the other, giving each one an equal amount of attention.

"Yeah! Yeah! Yeah!" Myah screamed as she was nearing her first orgasm.

Irk continue to finger her until she bucked up and down on his hand, letting loose what felt like a bucket full of pussy juice. He continued to move his fingers in and out until she stopped, and she said she wanted the real thing.

Before he could position himself to enter her, Myah pushed him back onto the bed, grabbed his rock hard dick in both hands, placed her soft plush lips on the head of it, and licked the pre-cum that was leaking out. She slid her mouth down past the tip and engulfed most of it, at the same time swirling her tongue around the head of his dick. Irk moaned as he tried to fight back the urge to explode inside of her mouth.

Myah moved herself so that she was directly between his legs, and moved her head up and down, faster and faster until she felt him twitch, which she knew was the sign that he was ready to cum. Instead of continuing, she stopped, lifted her mouth off of his dick, and stroked him in order to see him cum. She loved to watch the faces he made right before he released his nut.

"Oh shit! Ahhh, ahhh, ohhh! Yeah, that's it! Uhhh!" Irk moaned as jets of cum spewed from his dick onto her hand.

After a couple of more strokes, Myah put her lips back to his dick and sucked the rest of his nut into her mouth until he was limp. She never swallowed, and she wasn't about to start, so after she was done, she quietly got up off the bed, went into the bathroom and spit out what she had collected. When she finished, she flushed the toilet, rinsed out her mouth, then went back into the bedroom to finish what they had started.

After what seemed like hours, Myah and Irk were lying in bed, exhausted. "I don't know what it is, but every time I'm with you, I feel as if I'm drained of all my energy," Irk said as he laid on his back with his hands on his forehead.

Myah smiled, then turned to face him and replied, "It's this good ass snapper that's doing it to you."

They both laughed out loud until Myah's cell phone started ringing. It was in her coat pocket, which was laying on one of the chairs in the room. She jumped up to get it, but Irk grabbed her wrist and said, "Let it ring. Whoever it is will call back. If it's that important, they'll call back."

Myah did as she was told. She laid back down next to him, closed her eyes and felt a sense of comfort when he placed his arm around her to cuddle. She fell asleep with him breathing softly in her ear.

"Damn! Where's this bitch at?" Henry asked in an irritated tone of voice. He'd been trying to reach Myah for about an hour now, but with no luck. He was pissed that she wasn't answering her phone, especially since she knew that he was out and would be calling.

Henry was sitting in his apartment and smoking a blunt, trying to figure out his next move. It was ten p.m., and he was alone, wondering whether he should call Luscious up to get his nuts out of the dirt, but he just didn't want to be bothered with her attitude. Besides, he wanted something new; something fresh, and Myah was it. "Fuck it!" he said to himself, then closed the phone.

He got up off of the couch, looked around his apartment, and realized just how nice it really was. He looked over at the kitchen table and saw the two keys that Big O had given him, and decided to test it out for its purity. He took one of the bricks, peeled back the wrapping and tore a small hole in order to stick his finger in it. He scooped out a fingernail-full and sniffed it up his right nostril. It hit like a ton of bricks as soon as it went in. He knew right then that it wasn't stomped on at all. "Whew!" he said out loud as he shook his head from side to side. His eyes started to water, and the drainage started to make his throat numb. "Damn, that's some good shit!" *The coke that I was getting in prison was nowhere near as strong as this!* he thought to himself. Henry walked over to the kitchen sink, turned the faucet on and cupped his hands in order to catch some water to splash on his face, and to run up his nose.

Just as he was starting to enjoy the high, his cordless phone rang. It startled him at first, then he realized that it was just the phone ringing in the living room. No one knew his number except Luscious, and he didn't feel like having her come over. But he knew that if he didn't answer it, she would just keep calling until he did. He walked over to it, picked it up and pressed the on button. "Yeah!" he answered in a slurred voice. His tongue felt like sandpaper. It made his speech sound funny.

"Henry, you drunk?" Luscious asked in a concerned voice.

"What?"

"Have you been drinking? You sound funny."

"Nay, I'm just tired, that's all," he lied, trying to straighten out the sound of his voice.

"Well, I'm coming over, a'ight?"

Henry thought about it, then decided, what the fuck. He wasn't doing anything anyway. Plus, he was feeling a little horny. "Yeah, come on, and wear something nice for daddy."

Luscious smiled and knew just what to put on for him. "I'll be over in an hour. Let me get dressed." She hung up and went to her closet to find that schoolgirl outfit she had bought for some guy she was dating a while ago. While Henry waited, he put away the two keys, and counted out thirty thousand dollars to buy himself a whip. Since he was back, he had to let people know. "A hustler never stops hustling. He just takes breaks," was what he said as he put the twenty-thousand that was left away in his coat pocket.

His heart was racing from the coke, but Henry was used to it. It took a lot more than just a pinch of coke to affect him.

He sat down on his couch to watch some TV, but decided to call Myah one last time before Luscious arrived. The phone rang about three times before she finally answered it.

"Hello."

He fumbled for the right words to say. It was like déjà vu all over again. Somehow, he felt like he'd gone through this before. Then, he remembered thirteen years ago, that fine ass girl he had met at Club Bentley's before he got locked up.

"Hello!" Myah said once more, trying to figure out who was calling her at this time of night. She heard someone breathing, but wasn't sure if it was someone just playing, or if someone had called the wrong number. She was about to hang up when a voice answered.

"Yeah, what's up, baby girl?"

Myah couldn't believe it. It was Henry. After two days of being out, he finally decided to call. She was expecting it, but then again, she dreaded it at the same time. She went into Irk's bathroom and closed the door so that she could talk freely without waking him up. He was still sleeping after their lovemaking session. If it wasn't for the fact that she had to use the bathroom, she would still be asleep herself.

Once the door was closed, she sat on the toilet and started to pee, not caring if Henry heard or not. She cleared her throat and went into her, "I missed you!" routine. "Hey, baby! Why didn't you call me when you got out?"

"I wanted to get myself situated first. I had to see my parole officer before I could do anything. What'cha doin' tonight?"

Myah's mind raced to find an excuse, then came up with, "Oh, I'm about to go to one of the clubs downtown." Since he didn't know that she was in the Bronx, she played it off as if she was still at school. "Why? Where you at?"

"I'm in tha Bronx right now. When are you coming back this way?" he asked, wondering when he was going to be able to tap that ass of hers. His dick started to get hard as he thought about all the things that he wanted to do to her. But, before he could get deep into it, he heard the lock on his door clicking. His mind went into defensive mode, which caused him to jump up. "Hold on!" he told Myah as he put the phone down on the couch to see who was trying to come into his apartment.

He crept towards the front door and waited until the door opened. When he saw that it was Luscious, he snapped. "How tha fuck did you get a key to my apartment?"

Luscious jumped back once she saw Henry standing behind the door. Her heart was racing so fast that she thought she was going to have a heart attack. As soon as she gained her composure, she answered him. "Damn, baby! You scared the shit outta me! What you doing behind the door like that?"

"Fuck that! How the fuck did you get a key to my apartment?" he asked a second time, slamming the door shut.

"I had a set made when I leased it! Why are you yelling at me-e-e-e?" Luscious asked as she started to get scared when she saw the anger in his eyes.

Henry looked at her, then realized that Myah was still on the phone in the living room. "Wait right here!" he told Luscious as he ran back to get the phone. "Hello!"

"Yeah. Who the fuck is that?" Myah demanded to know. She couldn't hear everything, but she did hear a woman's voice.

Henry didn't know whether she heard what had gone down, but he didn't want her to think that he was with someone else and piss her off. "Ummm, just someone coming to say what's up. You know, people wanting to pay their respects to a thorough nigga." He saw Luscious walking into the room, and motioned for her to go into the bedroom. She did, only after making a face when she saw him on the phone. "Yeah. Let me call you right back after I get rid of these people, a'ight?"

"Just call me tomorrow after eleven. I should be up by then."

"You bet'cha. I'll holla at'cha." With that, Henry hung up and proceeded into his bedroom to finish cussing Luscious out some more.

The next day, after getting his morning nut before Luscious left him, Henry got out of bed and thought about what he had to do. He thought about how he was finally going to hook up with Myah. Every time he looked at her pictures in the joint, his dick got rock hard just thinking about what he would do. "I hope Bear is enjoying them," he said with a smile on his face right before he hopped his ass in the shower.

First order of business was to find a whip. Luscious had told him she would take him after she went back to her apartment in order to change into something more conservative than her schoolgirl outfit. Oh, did they have fun playing "Naughty Schoolgirl"! Henry always had a fetish with role-playing, and being that he was high on coke, they fucked all night until they finally passed out from sheer exhaustion.

Luscious knew that she wouldn't walk right in the morning, but she needed it just as much as he did.

Now, as he waited for her to pick him up, Henry thought about his son and that bitch, Libra. On the ride from prison, Luscious had informed him that Libra just upped and moved — no warning or anything. Henry knew why. She knew he would be looking for her trifling ass, so she disappeared. It didn't matter. After a few phone calls here and there, he found out that she was staying at her sister's house in New Jersey. He planned on paying her a visit just as soon as he got his shit together. He had to play it smart, since he knew that they would be watching him. "Restraining Order, my ass!" he said to himself. "That bitch can't hide from me!"

His thoughts were interrupted when he heard a car horn outside his window. He made a mental note to call his man, Jay Nizzle from KC, Missouri, who he met in the pen. *Yeah, that pretty muthafucka is Libra's type. She'll go for his ass!* Henry thought. *Little would she know that that innocent, clean-cut nigga is a stone cold killer!*

Luscious' car horn beeped a few more times before Henry looked out of the window and waved for her to hold on. He grabbed his jacket that had the thirty-thousand dollars in the pocket, and went out of his door to hop into Luscious' car.

"Yeah, I like that!" Luscious said excitedly as she looked inside of Henry's new SUV. They had gone out to Queens to a spot that Henry knew dealt with altered cars. He walked in and saw that the management had changed. Instead of seeing a familiar face, he was greeted by Arabs that looked as if they should be running a 7-Eleven. After seeing him pull out his stack of bills, they directed him to the garage, where they had a selection of brand new stolen SUV's that were in the process of being changed over to legit vehicles.

Henry saw a white metallic 2000 Lincoln Navigator with a light gray leather and wood grain interior. It was sitting on twenty-inch chrome Gianellis that made the truck stand out even more. As soon as he opened the door to look inside, he was shocked to see that the running boards slid out from underneath the truck in order for him to step up into it. "Damn!" was all he could say as he stepped up to inspect the plush interior.

Before he could even give it a test drive, he motioned for the Arab who was giving him the tour, to come closer. Once he did, Henry said in a low voice, "How much?"

The Arab thought about the price that he knew he could get for it, then smiled. "Twenty-five!" He knew that he was cutting it close if Henry knew about cars, especially about how stolen cars were sold.

Henry looked around the interior, then stated, "Twenty, and I want it today."

The Arab knew he would be a fool to pass that up, so when he saw Henry counting out the money, he smiled and said in his foreign accent, "Sold!"

Henry hopped out of the truck, handed him the bills,

then walked with the Arab to pick up the paperwork and the keys.

Luscious couldn't believe what she just saw. *He just got out of prison, and already he had one of the nicest trucks on the streets, while I'm driving a raggedy ass Subaru! Ain't that a bitch!* she thought to herself as she waited for him to come back.

Henry came out of the office, carrying an envelope and a set of keys. She walked over towards him, and once in front of him she asked, "Baby, where did you get that kind of money? You just got out of prison!"

Henry never liked for people to question him, especially someone like Luscious, but since he needed her to register the car in her name, he would have to be nice. "Some of my peoples looked out for me. It's a welcome home gift."

"I sure wish I had friends like that!" Luscious said in a sarcastic voice.

Henry turned around and said, "What?" He thought she had said something, but wasn't sure.

She didn't want to repeat it, so she just played it off. "I said, 'Damn!' You're doing it like that?'"

He turned back around and walked to the truck. He placed the temporary tags in the back window, then hopped in and started the engine.

Luscious waited to see what he was going to do before she went to her car.

"Follow me to Motor Vehicles. I want you to register it for me," Henry yelled from the driver side window.

Luscious nodded her head, then went to get into her car. She followed him out of the lot and into traffic, heading towards the Belt Parkway.

FIFTEEN

Detective Williamson was sitting in an unmarked gray Crown Victoria on the corner of Wellington and Bailey, trying to figure out Henry's next move. He just followed him from Queens, where he observed him buying a brand new truck from a known illegal car dealer. He then followed him to the Department of Motor Vehicles, where he assumed he went to get the truck registered.

After the young lady, whose name he learned was Lisa Taylor, known on the streets as Luscious, had left him, Henry then traveled back to the Bronx to where they were now. Williamson knew that eventually, Henry was going to slip up, and that's what everyone was banking on.

Since he was doing this without the authorization of the Department, Williamson knew that he couldn't officially do anything, unless he saw a blatant illegal act taking place. The little things that Henry was doing weren't enough for Detective Williamson to expose himself.

As he waited, he radioed to Detective Moody, who was in Trenton, New Jersey, watching the comings and goings of Libretta Nichols. "Detective Moody, see anything suspicious?"

Moody grabbed his police radio and pressed the button on the side to talk. "No, nothing out of the ordinary."

They hoped that Henry would be pissed off enough to get revenge for what he was put through, and for the death of his son. He made it adamantly clear while he was in court that he would get her back for lying on him. Now that he was back on the streets, they knew from talking to a few of his known victims that Henry was a man of his word.

"Well, he's back in the Bronx, so I guess you can head on home from there," Detective Williamson said into his radio as he watched a few people eye his vehicle suspiciously.

"Will do."

Detective Stevens was taking the day off. He was responsible for watching out for Myah. After learning that she was with Dirk Wright at his apartment in Soundview Project, Stevens headed back home to get some rest before he went back to work. Since the force made him take an early retirement, he picked up a job helping his cousin, who owned a small electronics shop. He was just doing it to keep busy. Now that he was "back on the job", even if it was unofficially, he had as much reason to put Henry back in prison as anyone else. The day that he went into his little rage, he struck Stevens in the chest with a bullet that caused him to have to retire earlier than expected.

Now, as he was driving over the Whitestone Bridge, he thought about all the things that Henry had taken away from him. "Yeah, muthafucka! You'll get yours! You'll get yours!" he said before getting off at his exit.

Henry looked out of the bedroom window of his

third floor apartment for the unmarked police car that had been following him all day. He took a pull of his Newport and thumped the ashes into an ashtray that was sitting on the windowsill. "I see you, muthafucka!" he said in a low voice as he eyed the top of the car's roof.

Even though he didn't know why they were following him, Henry decided to play with them. He knew that his apartment was clean, so he wasn't worried about that. The rest of his money was stashed safely in his coat pocket, so he wasn't concerned about them raiding his place. The only thing he could think of was that it was one of those two detectives that had shot him while he was at Libra's apartment building twelve years ago.

Henry started thinking of ways to get them back for what they had done to him, especially the older white one that shot him in the shoulder, which still bothered him to this day. He closed the curtain, sat on his couch, and finished the rest of his cigarette as he thought of ways to trick them out of their lives.

Henry pulled out the cell phone that Big O's man, Juicy had given him, pressed number one, then send, and waited for someone to answer.

After ringing three times, someone answered in a deep voice. "Yeah!"

Henry recognized it to be Juicy, and proceeded to talk. "Yeah, this is Henry. I need your assistance with something."

When Juicy realized who it was, he waved the young girl that was sucking his dick away, and waited for her to leave the room before he continued to talk. "What's the problem?"

After Henry explained the situation, Juicy told him that it would be taken care of, and hung up, leaving Henry on the other end with a grin on his face.

Twenty minutes had passed before Detective Williamson decided to call it a night. Henry hadn't left his apartment, and since it was getting late, he wanted to get back home before traffic got too heavy.

Before he started his car, a black '92 four door Honda Accord drove slowly past his vehicle. Right before it turned the corner, it came to a complete stop. Williamson only paid attention to it because it was out of place, especially in this type of neighborhood. He noticed that the driver was looking in his direction as if he was trying to see whether he knew him. After about thirty seconds of this stare-down, the car continued on, disappearing around the corner, out of Williamson's sight.

The whole thing seemed odd, but Williamson just shrugged it off and proceeded to start his car. The V-8 engine of the Crown Victoria came to life on the first try. He looked in his side mirror, then rearview to make sure he was okay to pull out. Just as he was about to switch the transmission into drive, a tap on his driver side window startled him. Shaken, he turned to see the same guy that he noticed earlier in the Honda, staring at him with a .357 on a 38 frame in his right hand, with the barrel pointed at his face.

Williamson ducked down in his seat just seconds before the first bullet shattered the driver side window. He tried to cover up when the shooter reached inside and fired a second shot that hit him in the back. In pain, Williamson reached under his seat to retrieve his Glock .40, but he was struck in the back of his head by another bullet. With the engine still running, he couldn't make out anything. A bright flash overtook him right before the shooter hit him with two more head shots.

The sound of gunfire was heard up and down the block, but no one dared look for fear that they would be seen, which was just what the shooter was hoping for. After he realized that the detective was dead, he tucked the gun into his sweatshirt and quickly ran around the corner to the car he had parked just minutes before. He hopped in, threw the gun on the passenger's seat, started the car and sped off down the block.

Detective Williamson's body laid across the front seat of his car, with one shot to his back, and three shots to his head. Brain matter was mixed in with the blood that covered the seat. Sirens could be heard in the distance, but everyone knew it was too late.

Henry was on the phone with Luscious when he heard the shots.

"What's that?" Luscious screamed into the receiver, causing Henry to pull the phone away from his ear. "Damn, bitch! Stop screaming in my ear! It's probably someone shooting off their gun." But he knew it was more than that. He got up off the couch and walked over to the window. He looked in the direction of where the unmarked car was, and saw a tall dark figure leaning inside of the car's driver side window. A bright flash lit up the interior, then another. The sound of the shots was deafening even from three floors up.

Henry closed the curtain and smiled. He knew that whomever it was, was doing exactly what he wanted done.

"Oh my God! I knew I should have gotten you another place somewhere else!" he heard Luscious say after the fourth shot was heard.

"Shit! It could happen anywhere," Henry stated as he sat back down. "Yo, let me call you back in a few." He hung up the phone, grabbed his jacket from out of his coat closet, and went out of the door to see whether it was one of the detectives that had sent him to prison who just got their life taken.

Nikki was watching her favorite show on TV when it was interrupted by the stations' news:

> "*This just in. Detective C.T. Williamson of the 43rd Precinct was found murdered in the lower east side of the Bronx about an hour ago.*" (A photograph of the slain detective was shown, along with a short bio.) "*Our prayers go out to his friends and family...*"

Nikki was just about to go into the kitchen when she heard the detective's name. When she saw his picture on the screen, she immediately gasped and covered her mouth. "That's Myah's friend! Oh my God!" She reached into the pocket of her jacket, grabbed her cell phone, pressed the memory for Myah's number and waited for her to answer. "Come on! Come on!"

After the phone rang five times, Myah's voice mail came on, causing Nikki to curse out loud. "*Fuck!*" She hung up, then tried again, hoping that Myah would pick it up out of irritation. "Answer the damn phone, Myah! Answer the phone—"

"Hello!" Myah answered in a sleepy voice, which caught Nikki off guard.

"Myah, where are you?"

"What? What's wrong, Nikki? You sound upset."

"Shit! I was watching my show when they interrupted it with a breaking news flash. Your friend, that detective we went to see a few months ago..."

"Yeah, what about him?" Myah asked as she sat up in Irk's bed. Irk was gone when she woke up, so she was all alone in his apartment.

"Well, they said that he just got killed somewhere in the Bronx. It's all over the news right now. Where are you?" Nikki screamed into the phone frantically.

"*Oh my God, no!* Why, why, *why?*" Myah continued to ask over and over again.

Nikki started to cry, because she heard Myah crying. "Myah, where are you?"

"I'm over at Irk's. I'm leaving right now!" Myah hung up with Nikki, hopped out of bed, found her clothes and quickly slipped them on. It took her no more than five minutes to get herself together before she left Irk's apartment, and headed for her car which was parked in front of his building.

Not caring what she looked like, she took the elevator to the lobby, and went straight out of the front door with tears in her eyes. She found her car, hit the button on her key chain to deactivate her alarm system, hopped behind the steering wheel and started the engine. She pulled away from the curb, and headed for the Throgs Neck Bridge to go home. On the entire drive there, she thought about her and Williamson's conversation, which made her cry even more. "Why, why, why?" was all she could say over and over again.

SIXTEEN

Williamson's murder sparked a statewide manhunt for the killer or killers. No one saw or heard anything. There were no suspects, and police everywhere were making it hard for anyone to eat illegally.

Irk's business was hit the hardest because of the constant presence of the "Boys in Blue". New York's finest were everywhere, as they continued to canvas the projects in hopes of turning up a witness or suspect.

Henry laid low throughout, waiting it out until the heat died down. He continually tried to get in touch with Myah, who was not answering her phone. After the third day of calling her, he gave up, and as he wondered about why she was avoiding him, she was back in Long Island with her aunt and uncle, grieving over the loss of a good friend.

As they watched the funeral on TV, Myah thought about her first and only visit to Williamson's office, and how he tried to explain his theory of who he thought

murdered her mother. After she finished watching the
funeral, she went to her room and laid on her canopy bed,
closed her eyes, and made a promise that she would make
it right. She would even the score. "Tit-4-Tat, muthafucka!
Tit-4-Tat!"

Her thoughts were focused on one thing, and one
thing only; bringing down the one person she knew was
responsible for her mother's death. Somehow, she felt that
Henry had something to do with Detective Williamson's
murder as well. She was starting to believe that everyone
she felt was close to her was starting to get affected by her
obsession for revenge.

Myah was ready to put her plan into motion, but she
knew she would have to face her demons if she was to be
successful.

That night, Myah dreamt of the night that she walked
to her mother's room and saw Henry beating her mother
repeatedly while at the same time raping her. The look on
his face as he thrusted himself in and out of her lifeless
body brought a chill to her that went bone deep.

As she tossed and turned during the night, Henry's
face continued to haunt her thoughts. For twelve years,
that face has caused many of sleepless nights for Myah.

Each time she dreamt of that day, she always woke
up with more hatred in her heart for him. Now that he was
finally out, she could finally put her plan of revenge into
action. But for some reason, Myah knew that she wasn't
prepared.

The next morning, Myah awoke to her alarm buzzing
on her nightstand beside her bed. She stretched, then
hopped out of her bed and went straight to the bathroom.
After splashing cold water on her face, she went back into
her room and looked for her cell phone, which she left in
her Coach bag. It had been there for three days, and as she

listened to her voice mail, there were umpteen messages, mostly from Henry.

After she listened to about three of them, she decided to set up a time and place for them to finally meet. She punched in his phone number and waited for him to answer. She looked at her clock and saw that it was just past eight, and didn't care if she was waking him up. All she had on her mind now was how she was going to trick him into trusting her.

As Henry looked into his bathroom mirror, he thought about what his face-to-face with Myah was going to be like without the guards watching their every move. His dick got hard thinking about how good she looked whenever she came to visit him in those sexy outfits, and how good she looked in the pictures she sent to him while he was in prison. He was finally going to be able to touch her in more ways than one.

He was in such a trance that he almost forgot that he had to hop his ass in the shower and get dressed if he was going to meet her on time. "Why does she want to meet me at the mall instead of at her crib or mine?" he asked himself as he pulled down his boxers.

Henry hesitated for a few seconds longer, admiring his physique, then walked over to the shower and stepped in.

Libra hadn't heard from or seen Henry since he's been out, but she was still being cautious of her surroundings. She didn't put it past him to just pop up when she least expected it, which was why she never left her sister's house too often.

Her sister, Egypt, who was slightly taller than she was, and stacked like a brick house, was tired of playing homebody ever since Libra came to live with her. She was used to hitting the clubs and hanging with large crowds, which she hadn't done in a while. But tonight, she was going to a club in Manhattan that they've never been to, that her girlfriend, Debra had heard about.

"Gi-r-r-rl, my cousin's boyfriend knows the owner, and he told him to bring some nice looking girls, so she asked me to find four friends to come. We'll have the VIP treatment, and the whole nine yards!" Debra said excitedly over the phone as she walked through her living room, heading towards the kitchen.

Debra was a 5'2" bombshell, with hazel colored eyes, long curly black hair, a small waist, and an ass that made niggas say, *"Damn!"* whenever they saw her. All of her friends called her "Baby Doll" because of her height. But guys called her "China Doll" because whenever she got high, her eyes would look chinky after she got fucked up, giving her that exotic Oriental look. Together with her thick thighs and busty chest, she was a bona fide dime piece.

Egypt didn't need her arm twisted. An opportunity to mingle with some power players at a new hot spot was all she needed, so she quickly said yes to the invite. Then, after hanging up with Debra, she ran upstairs to tell her sister that they were going to get out of the house tonight, whether she liked it or not.

Club Evolutions was the spot to be in. Everyone was either trying to get in, or was already in there, and having a good time. The line at the door was around the block, as people waited in their leather jackets or fur coats. The dress code was casual, and no sneakers or boots were allowed inside. Opening night was expected to be packed, and once capacity reached 700, the bouncers were ordered to stop admittance until further notice. People pulled up in Bentleys, Limos, Porsches, BMW's, Mercedes Benz's and other luxury cars, which were valet parked by the dozen or so parking attendants.

Egypt, Libra, Debra, Tamara and Kizsme were all dressed to kill, and they knew it. Debra's cousin, Tamara, led them around to the VIP door, and told the bouncer that their names were on this list, which he checked quickly, then allowed them to go in. Once inside, all eyes were on them as they made their way up the winding staircase that led to the VIP room.

A steady stream of beautiful women were walking around as if they were on display for all to see. *It's definitely a fashion show,* Libra thought to herself as she and her entourage made their way to one of the many plush couches that surrounded the room.

Champagne bottles were on every table, and once they were emptied, waiters supplied fresh ones in ice buckets. The men were either ballers, or someone of importance, as people catered to their every need.

Libra was wearing a black Dolce & Gabana one piece form fitting dress, a pair of sheer black stockings, along with a pair of six-inch black, open toed stilettos, which made her look taller than five-four. Her sister and the rest of her crew were equally dressed to impress.

When they were all seated at an empty table, waiters came over to take their orders. "Hello, ladies. Can I interest you in something to drink?" a tall, dark skinned brother, wearing a white button down shirt and black slacks, asked in a pleasant voice.

The music wasn't as loud inside the soundproof room as it was inside the club, so no one had to yell or shout out their orders. Conversation and laughter was all that could be heard, as everyone mingled and had a good time. The atmosphere was relaxing, which made Libra loosen up a bit as she looked around the room and eyed a couple of fine brothers staring at her from across the room. The club was definitely jumping, which was evident by the many people moving about.

"I'll have a sex on the beach," Tamara said with a smile.

Debra looked over at her and said, "Oh no you won't! We'll have a bottle of champagne, and five glasses please, if you don't mind."

"No problem. Will that be all?" the waiter asked as he leaned down a little to hear Debra.

"Yes. Thank you."

After he was gone, Debra smiled, then turned towards Egypt. "Aren't you glad that you came, girl?"

"Hell yeah! Just look at all these fine ass niggas up in here!"

Everyone looked around and agreed that there were some good looking brothers up in the club tonight. Even Libra had to smile a little as she continued to scope out the large, glass-enclosed room that overlooked the dance floor below.

A group of brothers strolled by their table, stopping briefly to converse, then continued on to wherever they were going. As the girls were commenting on them, the tall, light skinned brother that was eyeing Libra earlier came over, stood on the side of her and said, "Excuse me. I don't mean to bother you, but I had to come over here and find out your name. Ever since I saw you walk in, I couldn't take my eyes off of you."

Libra was taken aback by his boldness, especially

since he walked up to a table full of fine women that could easily have any one of the many men in there. She turned to face him, and even though she knew what he looked like from afar, up close he was even more attractive. His hair was cornrowed straight to the back, and his dark brown eyes were captivating. He was wearing a powder blue Giorgio Brutini suit, with a pair of powder blue and white Cole Haan Edwin capped toed crocodile shoes. He stood about 6'2, and weighed at least 225. Libra was speechless as he waited for her to respond.

Egypt took it upon herself to tell him Libra's name. "Her name is Libretta, Libra for short. And yours is?"

"Oh, I'm sorry, ladies. I'm usually not so rude. My name is Jay, but my friends all call me Jay Nizzle."

"Well, it's nice to meet you, Jay—Jay Nizzle. I'm Egypt, this is Debra, Tamara, and over here is Kizsme. You already know Libra. Would you like to have a seat, Jay?"

"Sure. I would love to," he answered as he stepped around the couch in order to sit next to Libra. The whole time he was doing so, he never took his eyes off of her. "Can I buy you ladies something to drink?"

Just as he asked them that question, the waiter came back with their champagne and five glasses. "Oh, I didn't know you were having company. Would you like a glass also, sir?"

Jay looked at the table, then said, "Yes, if it's not too much trouble. I would like you to send me the check for whatever these fine ladies order. It's on me!" he stated as he looked at Libra and smiled.

The waiter excused himself once again and left. Everyone was smiling as they thanked Jay.

"It's my pleasure."

Libra was definitely impressed by how this young baller was handling himself.

After the waiter came back with his glass, Jay poured everyone a glass of Dom, and they toasted to having a good night. Everyone was having a good time, especially when some other fine men came over and asked the other girls if they wanted to dance, which they did, in order to give Libra and Jay some time alone. Once they were, Jay told Libra all about himself, and she did the same. After three more glasses of champagne, Libra was feeling no pain. In fact, she was starting to feel a little too good, which was not lost on Jay Nizzle. "Would you like to get some air, Libra? You look a little hot."

"That's a good idea. Will we be able to get back in if we leave?" Libra asked with concern.

"I'm sure we will. I know the bouncers at the door. I'm sure it wouldn't be a problem," he added as he stood up and waited for her to come from around the couch.

"Maybe I should tell my sister that I'll be right back."

"Will you be alright?" Jay asked in a concerned voice.

Libra looked into his eyes and smiled as she thought that he was the finest brother in the place. "Yeah, I'll be alright. I'll just be a minute." She turned around and tried to walk, but the champagne was fucking with her equilibrium. "Oh my! I guess I do need a helping hand. I didn't think I had that much to drink."

Jay put his arm around her small waist and guided her out of the VIP door, down the stairs and towards her sister, who was grinding her fat ass into the young brother that she was dancing with. Jay led her next to them, and let Libra talk to her sister while he conversed with the young baller, who thought he was doing something.

"I'm gonna go out for a minute to get some fresh air, a'ight?"

"Gir-r-r-l, you need to get some fresh dick! If you

don't let that fine muthafucka tap that ass of yours, then I will!" Egypt said with a smile.

"Bitch, please! You would still let him even if I did!"

They both laughed as Jay came over to them and placed his arm around Libra's neck, making her feel safe. "I'll take care of her, don't worry."

"You better do more than that!" Egypt added with a smirk on her face as she made her way back to the young brother that she was dancing with earlier. "Be safe!" she said before turning around.

Libra and Jay made their way through the crowded dance floor and out of the door with no problems. Once they were in the cool night air, Libra let out a breath and commented on how nice it was. "So, Jay, are you still having a good time?"

"As long as I'm with you, I am."

"That so nice of you to say." Libra looked around and noticed that people were still lined up to get in. She glanced at her watch and saw that it was going on one-thirty in the morning. "Wow! This place is still packing them in even at this time of the morning!"

Jay looked around, and once he realized that no one was paying them any mind, he decided to ask Libra a question. "Hey, would you like to grab something to eat with me before we go back in. The place doesn't close until five, and I'm sure your friends aren't going to leave before then," he added, once he saw how she was looking.

"I am kind'a hungry. Maybe that'll help me to sober up a little, huh?"

"It wouldn't hurt, and I promise to behave myself."

They both laughed as Jay waved to get the valet's attention. Once one of them came over, Jay gave him his ticket and waited for the young valet to bring his car around. A shiny mint green four door 745I BMW emerged from the parking lot and stopped in front of them.

Libra's eyes grew big as she saw Jay open the door for her to get in. "Your chariot awaits!" he said with a smile. Libra hopped into the passenger's seat, and after Jay closed the door, he walked around to the driver's side, slipped the valet attendant a ten, then jumped behind the wheel, closed the door, and drove off down the street.

The interior of the car was plush. The seats were made of butter-soft tan leather. The paneling on the door, dashboard and steering wheel were dark wood grain. It was so spacious inside, that Libra felt as if she was sitting in a living room.

As he drove, Jay pressed a button on the steering wheel, and a six and a half-inch screen folded out from the stereo receiver, which bought the stereo to life. The sound of soft jazz played in the many speakers that surrounded the interior of the car. "I hope you like soft jazz," Jay said as he looked over at her.

"Oh, that's fine." Libra was really feeling Jay's style. *If this keeps up, I'ma definitely give him some of this pussy!* She thought. Just the thought of it made her pussy get wet as she crossed her legs in order to control herself.

Jay saw the way she was fidgeting, and smiled. He knew that she was feeling him, which was why he was chosen. He spotted a small restaurant a few blocks away, and saw that they were still open. He found a place to park, and once the engine was off, he got out, walked around to Libra's door, and opened it for her.

He's a perfect gentleman, she thought as she stepped out of the car.

They walked inside and sat down at an empty table, and waited for someone to take their orders.

When they finished their breakfast, they sat and talked. "So, are you ready to head back?" Libra asked after she looked at her watch.

Jay smiled, and said, "If that's what you want to do."

Libra heard the hesitation in his voice. "What's wrong, Jay?"

"I was just thinking that I really don't want this night to end."

"It doesn't have to," she said in a low, seductive voice.

"Well, why don't we go find a hotel? I can take you back afterwards."

Libra thought for a second, then threw caution to the wind and said okay.

Jay paid the bill, got up and helped Libra to her feet. Then they walked out hand-in-hand, back to his car.

"Oh my God! That was incredible! I haven't felt like that in a long time!" Libra exclaimed after having her third orgasm.

Jay was looking at her as she laid in the bed, trying to catch her breath. They had just finished fucking, and after he busted his nut, he rolled off and pulled the condom that he had used off. He dug into his pants pocket, found his Newports, took out two and gave her one.

"Oh, thank you!"

Jay placed the lighter to her cigarette and lit it. As they laid there enjoying their cigarettes, he started talking. "You know, when I first saw you, I said to myself, *Damn! I have to have her!*"

Libra smiled and turned to look at him. It was as if he was too good to be true.

"Then, once I had the chance to finally talk to you, I felt bad."

Libra's smile disappeared as confusion took over.

"What?"

Jay continued to puff on his cigarette as she stared up towards the ceiling. "Yeah-h-h-h, I felt bad because I knew that after tonight, I wouldn't see you anymore."

Libra started to sit up as she dumped the ashes into the ashtray that was on the nightstand next to her bed. "Why aren't you going to be able to see me anymore?"

Jay placed his cigarette in the ashtray, leaned over to reach for his jacket, and pulled out a Swiss blade.

Libra couldn't make out what he was doing, but once Jay turned back around to face her, she saw the shiny blade of the knife. "Jay, what's that for?" she asked with fear in her voice.

"Oh, this? This here is what you call a 'knife'. It's good for all sorts of things."

The look in his eyes made Libra cringe. She moved back away from him, trying to put distance between her and what he had in his hand. She wanted to scream, but didn't want to jump to any conclusions. "Jay, you're scaring me! Can you please put that away?"

Jay smiled, leaned closer to her and said, "Henry wanted me to pay you back for everything you did to him."

When Libra heard Henry's name, her eyes got as large as saucers. Before she could scream, Jay pounced on her, held her mouth with his free hand, a brought the sharp blade of the knife straight across her throat, opening up a large gash. Libra tried to get free, but as the blood spurted from the cut, she felt too weak to even struggle. Jay continued to hold her down until he felt her go limp. Her eyes started to gloss over as death crept into her.

"Yeah, don't fight it, just accept it. Henry sends his love... *bitch!*"

The last thing Libra heard before she died was, "... And say hello to Henry Jr., you trifling *bitch!*"

SEVENTEEN

Myah and Henry's first face to face didn't go the way he thought it would. He thought that since he was finally out, she would have been eager to sex him down. But as it turned out, she played him to the left. As he continued to press for the pussy, she continued to stall for more time. Her reason for not wanting to was because she was on her period, which was also why she didn't answer her phone for three days. But before they went their separate ways, she did promise him that he would be able to sample her goodies very soon. She even promised to suck his dick, since she knew that he liked that from reading the letters he wrote her from prison.

That satisfied Henry a little, but for some reason, he kept thinking that she looked familiar to him, as if he had met her before. As quickly as that thought came, it went just as fast, leaving him confused. Since they were in the mall, he didn't want to cause a scene, so he left it at that and moved on once she disappeared out the front doors.

While they were having their little meeting, two of Irk's soldiers recognized Myah, and watched closely, trying to figure out if their man's girl was playing the field.

"While the cat's away, the mouse will play!" was what R.J. said to Pee-Wee as they waited in one of the stores that was situated to where Myah and Henry were sitting down, talking.

"Yo! Homeboy looks pissed about something, kid?" Pee Wee stated in a joking manner.

"Word! Oh, what tha fuck?" Did you see that, son?" R.J. asked excitedly as he spotted Myah touching Henry's face in a loving way.

"Who's this herb ass nigga, yo?"

"I don't know, nigga. All I know is that Irk's gon' be pissed like a muthafucka!" R.J. replied. "Yo, we should follow dude to see where he's from so that Irk can either murk old boy, or teach him a lesson about messing with other people's property."

"Oh yeah! O.P.P., huh? I'm with that!"

When they saw Henry begin to move, they followed him out of the mall and watched him jump into a clean ass Navigator and take off. They got into Pee-Wee's '99 burnt orange drop top Ford Mustang, and followed after him. Once they realized that he was headed around their way, they started wondering just who this nigga really was.

Henry parked his truck in front of his apartment building, got out, and went into the front door. R.J. and Pee-Wee parked a couple of cars down and watched Henry disappear into the building, which they recognized to be the Terrance Avenue Apartments. "Yo, this nigga must really be balling, or his peoples are," Pee-Wee exclaimed theatrically, making R.J. laugh a little.

"Yo, son, we should go holla at Irk before he leaves. Get him on the horn."

"Yes sir!" Pee-Wee dialed Irk's cell phone and waited for him to answer.

"Ayo! What's up?" Irk answered in a cheery voice.

"Ayo, Irk, this is Pee-Wee."

"What's going on, youngin' I know you ain't calling just to say what's up, so spit, little nigga!" he demanded.

"Yo, check this out! Me and R.J. were at the mall, and we saw your girl..."

"Yeah, so what?" Irk interrupted, trying to hurry the story along.

"...And she was all touchy-feely with a nigga!" Pee-Wee stopped to see if Irk was going to say that he already knew about it, but when he didn't, he cautiously continued. "Well, since they were all up on each other, we decided to follow homeboy just to see where he rest at, you know. And comes to find out that duke lives in the Terrace Ave. Apartments. We're here right now. What'cha wanna do?" he finished excitedly, as if he was trying to boost himself up.

Irk thought for a minute, then said, "He's there with her right now?"

"Nah. He's by himself. She left him at the mall."

"Come on back here. Don't forget that nigga's face, a'ight?" I might have to find his ass later if I don't like the answers I get. You hear me, my nigga?" Even though Irk felt betrayed, he couldn't show any signs of weakness.

Pee-Wee hung up, and while he and R.J. were on their way back to the block, Irk called Myah's cell just to see if all he heard was true.

Henry received a phone call as soon as he opened his apartment door. He looked at his watch and saw that it was going on eleven-forty. "Yeah, what's up?" he answered, hoping that it wasn't Luscious.

"It's done, my nigga," the voice on the other end said

in a monotone voice.

At first, Henry was confused. Then, after a couple of seconds, he recognized the caller. "Was it painful?"

"Yeah. You know my work."

"Did she know why?"

"For sure!"

Henry smiled. "Good! Good!" He walked over towards the window to see if the car that had followed him from the mall was still there. "Get ghost, my nigga. I'll be in touch."

"This one's on me. Welcome home, big homie! Be easy," the voice stated before hanging up.

Henry closed the curtains, then placed the phone on the table. He knew it would be a matter of time before he read of Libra's demise.

Tony was on the phone with one of the members of his group, as he walked towards his brand new black on black Lexis coupe. Since his group was doing so well in the record sales, he decided it was about time that he treated himself. He went out with Tania and picked out a new car to celebrate their success.

Just as he was about to hang up, two guys walked past him. Normally, he wouldn't have paid them any attention, but when he heard one of them say a name he hadn't heard in years, he tuned in.

"...Yeah, they say that that nigga's name used to ring bells around here a while back..."

Even though Tony wasn't sure if they were talking about the same person he was thinking about, just hearing the name brought him back to '89 and what had happened.

The two guys were about to turn the corner when

Tony decided to stop them. "Ayo!"

They looked back to see whether it was them being called. Once they realized that he was calling them, they turned around.

Tony met them half-way and said, "Yo, I don't mean to get in y'all's conversation, but I couldn't help it. Were y'all talking about a guy named Henry?"

The taller one spoke up first. "Who's you?"

Tony looked at the both of them, then said, "Oh, I'm Tony. I'm the manager of the group, The Potheadz."

The shorter one's eyes got big as he recognized Tony from the many magazine articles he read about the group. "Yeah, yeah, yeah! I know who you are. Your group's on fire, son! Word is bond!"

"Thanks. They're only gonna get better, believe me," Tony stated.

"So, you know Hen-Dog?" the taller one asked inquisitively.

Tony never heard that name before, but he played it off as if he knew who they were talking about. "Yeah, I knew him from back in the days, though. Like in '89, before he got locked up."

"Yeah, yeah, that's that nigga! Word on the streets is that he's looking for a few good men to make that paper. When he was out, he used to be 'that dude', so now he's trying to reclaim his 'hood, and they say that he's hungry!" the shorter one said excitedly.

Tony looked around, then back at the two guys in front of him, and said, "I heard that! There should be enough to go around, though."

"Nah, that nigga, Irk isn't about to let anyone eat unless it's him. It's gonna be problems, mark my word, son!" the taller man stated. "My name is Best, and I'm staying outta that mess! Word is bond!"

The two started walking off, leaving Tony standing by himself. Once they were gone, he walked back to his car, got in and drove off, thinking that he now has the chance to do what he should have done twelve years ago.

Across town, Irk and his entourage were standing around Zo's pearl white on white, fully loaded Range rover, discussing the potential problem that he was hearing about, which was what was going on in the streets.

"The streets are talking. The word is that some nigga is trying to push major weight in our spots. Now, I don't know about you, but I'm ready to handle this nigga proper like, you heard!" one of Irk's lieutenants was saying as he puffed on his second blunt.

"Who is this nigga anyway? Does this nigga have a name?" Irk asked angrily.

Lil' Dee, who controlled the lower west side, cleared his throat, then began to speak. "From what I heard, this nigga's trying to recruit some people to work with him. A kid I know told me that dude's name used to ring bells around here in the 80's. But he disappeared for a hot minute."

"Did your man get his name?" Zo asked, interrupting Lil' Dee's story.

"Yeah. Dude's name is Hen-Dog. He used to be about that paper, from what I heard of him."

"I don't give a fuck what homeboy's about! He ain't coming up in my 'hood, pushing a got-damn thing unless I say so! Does anyone know where this nigga rest at?"

"Nah. All I know is that he drives a bad ass white Navigator."

Irk's eyes grew wide as he thought back to what one

of his little soldiers was telling him earlier. *"Dude lives in the Terrace Ave. Apartments, and drives a white Navigator." Could this be the same nigga that they were talking about now?* Irk thought to himself as his people talked around him. "Yo, go check this out! Holla at Pee-Wee when he gets here, and see if that's the same nigga that he had followed earlier. I have to go see someone real quick. Hit me on the cell when you hear from him, a'ight?"

Zo acknowledged him with a head nod before Irk jumped into his own car and drove off, leaving everyone wondering where he was going in such a hurry.

EIGHTEEN

Myah was on the cell phone talking to Nikki while driving back to school, when she heard her phone beep, indicating that someone was trying to call her. "Hey, Nikki, hold on. I got another call."

"Well, hurry up! I wanna hear the rest of the story!" Nikki said, laughing.

Myah clicked over, making sure Nikki was off before saying, "Hello!"

As soon as Irk heard her voice, he said, "Hey, princess! Where you at?"

"Oh, hey, baby! I'm on my way back to school. I'm just about to get on the Thruway. Why, is something wrong?"

Irk tried to sound calm, but he couldn't hide the anger in his voice. "Yo, I have to ask you something, and I want you to tell me the truth."

Myah's mind started racing, trying to figure out why Irk sounded so mad. "What is it, baby?"

"Were you at the mall today?"

"Yeah. Why?" she asked, bewildered.

"Who were you with?"

Myah knew that no one saw her that he knew, so she

decided to lie. "No one. I went in real quick and picked up some new sneakers. I probably stayed about twenty minutes, then I was out. Is something wrong?"

Irk knew that she was lying. His peoples wouldn't make up anything, knowing how he would react. He played it off as if he was just asking. "Oh, I was just asking. Since I couldn't reach you, I just thought maybe you were at the mall or something. Give me a call once you get to your dorm, a'ight?"

"Sure. I love you, baby!" Myah said in a sweet sounding voice before she clicked back over to Nikki.

After hanging up with Myah, Irk was fuming at the thought that his girl was creeping around. After all that he had done for her, she had the audacity to fuck around on him! He was convinced more than ever that something was up. "If Pee-Wee tells me that the nigga he followed earlier is the same nigga that's causing him problems in the streets, I'ma see him myself! I swear on everything I love, homeboy is dead!" He said out loud as he clenched his fist, not realizing that he was squeezing his cell phone until he heard a cracking sound, which caused him to relax his hand.

Myah clicked back over to Nikki, who made her feel guilty for having her wait so long. "Bitch! I know you didn't just have me waiting that damn long!" she yelled into the phone bitterly.

"That was Irk. He sounded funny. He asked me some questions, as if he was being possessive or something."

"I told you that boy isn't no good! You need to cross over for good and leave them little boys alone."

They both laughed, as Myah drove the rest of the way to her school, thinking about what Irk said. *"I want you to tell me the truth."* It was as if he knew something already.

Once Myah was in her dorm room, she saw a note on her desk from her roommate:

> *I'll be back on Tuesday. I had something to do at home.*
>
> *Love ya!*

Myah crumpled the note up and threw it in the wastepaper basket. She thought to herself as she placed her bags of clothes on the floor, that she needed to sleep for at least ten hours. She was drained from the long drive up, and plus, she knew that Nikki would be over soon. She flopped on her bed, kicked off her boots, and curled up to go to sleep. She was so exhausted that it took her no time at all to fall asleep.

Something in her dream must have disturbed her, because when she awoke, she was breathing hard and shaking. Just when she was about to get out of bed, her cell phone began to ring.

Henry watched as the burnt orange Mustang drove off. He went into his bedroom and pulled out the shoebox that held some of the letters and pictures of Myah, the ones he didn't give to his homie, Bear. Something kept bothering him about her that he just couldn't shake off. As he pulled one of the pictures out of an envelope, he looked at it and thought back to what his man, Ed Ski, had said

when he first saw them. *"You don't even know this broad...
Look at her eyes... All of the pictures tell a serious story... She
had been betrayed or hurt really badly by someone before..."*

Henry continued to stare at one picture in particular.
Something about her eyes gave him the feeling that he
knew her from someplace.

"O-o-o-oh shit!" Suddenly, it all came back to him.
He now knew why she looked so familiar to him. "Myah
Johnson! What was that bitch's name? Tonya... no, no
no... something, something... Sonya Johnson! That's it!
That's who she looks like! Oh shit! This bitch been playing
me the whole time! Imagine that! Okay, bitch, you wanna
play games? Well, this is one game you'll definitely lose, I
promise you that!"

Henry was furious. He threw the pictures back into
the shoebox and continued to rant and rave. "You started
this shit, but I'm gonna finish it!" Now his mind was racing
to figure out how he was going to deal with "Little Miss
I wanna get even". "Bitch! You done jumped into a pond
where I'm the big fish!"

Just as he was in deep thought, his house phone
started ringing, bringing him back to reality. Henry let it
ring two more times before he answered it. "Yeah, who's
this?"

"Henry, they found Libra's body in a Manhattan hotel
last night! They say that she's been dead for about two days
now. Her throat was cut. Can you believe that?" Luscious
said excitedly as she read the newspaper article again.

Henry smiled, knowing that his man did the dirty
deed. "Oh yeah? I guess the bitch got what she deserved,"
he said with no sympathy in his voice.

"Henry! How could you say that? You had nothing
to do with that, right? Tell me you had nothing to do with
that, please!" she pleaded.

Henry thought about it, then decided that the less she knew, the better. "Hell no! Why would you even say some dumb shit like that over the damn phone anyway?"

"I'm sorry. I was just..."

"You were just, what? Thinking that since I hated her for what she did to me and my son that I had something to do with it, right? Well, I ain't no killer!"

Luscious knew how revengeful he could be, but she never knew him to be a killer. "I just don't want you to get caught up again. When can I come see you?"

"Let me take care of some things today, and I'll give you a call later, a'ight?"

"You better call me, Henry, as soon as you finish! I miss it, baby!" she said in a seductive tone, which turned him on.

"When I do, you better be wet and ready!" he replied, knowing that she would be.

After they said their good-byes, he then went back to his bedroom to pack a few things for the trip he was about to take. He decided to pay Myah a visit up at her school. He was going to find out just how much she really knew about that night he killed her mother.

"Yeah, hello!" Myah answered her cell phone on the fourth ring.

"Myah, I hope I'm not interrupting you or anything, but I need to talk to you as soon as possible," the voice said in a hurried tone.

Myah was confused. She thought it was Nikki calling, but once she heard the male voice, her mind went into defensive mode. "Okay, but first, *who the hell is this?*" At first, she didn't recognize the voice, but once he said his name, she quickly apologized for being so rude to him.

"Don't worry about it. Listen! I need to see you. I really can't talk over the phone. Your school is in Potsdam, New York, right?"

"Yeah, why?"

"Well, I'm on the Thruway right now, and I'm programming my GPS for your location. All I need is your dorm and room number."

Myah couldn't believe what she was hearing. She didn't know how to respond, so she just went ahead and gave him the information he needed. "I live in Lawrence Hall, room 215. How long will it take you to get here?"

"I should be there in about seven hours, tops. I'll call before I get into town to let you know," Tony said, trying to sound calm.

"Tony, what does this have to do with?"

Tony thought about it, then said, "Let's just say it has to do with our past."

"I'll be waiting," Myah replied, then hung up.

Irk was determined to get to the bottom of who exactly was the guy that Myah was seen with. Even though he was never the jealous type, he had to know who would have the balls to even fuck with one of his. In a sense, he was hurt since he treated Myah like a queen ever since that first day they saw each other in the pizza shop. He never meant for it to turn into an intimate relationship, but now that they were together, he found it hard to let go.

As he was heading back to the block, he received a call from Big Zo, informing him that the guy that was trying to open up shop in his 'hood was, in fact, the same person that was at the mall with Myah. Not only was he trying to cut into Irk's money, he was also trying to get with Irk's main girl.

Irk told Zo to meet him at his crib in order for him to be picked up. Irk was dead set on confronting old boy face to face to see for himself who he was, and just what his intentions were.

After picking up Zo in front of his projects, they drove over to the Terrance Avenue Apartments, with the sole purpose of talking. Now, if homeboy decided to get out of line, Irk planned on straightening his ass out with the Glock-9 that he had under his seat, and the .45 that was under his arm in a holster, just in case they couldn't see eye to eye. Zo was packing his twins; two nickel plated .380's that were a gift from Irk. Irk didn't want to bring the crew for the simple fact that he didn't think he would need them.

Just as they were pulling up in front of the apartments, Zo spotted a dark figure walking towards a white Navigator, the same one that Pee-Wee described that homeboy drove, and who was with Myah at the mall.

Irk drove past slowly in order to get a better look at old boy. There was something about him that he recognized. He searched his mind to find out where he had seen him before. Then he remembered that he was that nigga that caught that rape charge on his girl, and tried to take out three cops when they came to arrest him. "Oh shit!" Irk said in a low voice as he eyed Henry in his rearview mirror.

"What?" Zo asked suspiciously.

"I know that nigga! Remember back in the day when that nigga had a shootout with the police when they tried to arrest him after he raped his girl in her apartment?"

"Nah. When was this?" Zo asked, trying to think.

"Back in '89."

"Oh, yeah! Homeboy made the news and all. They

tried to pin a murder on him too, but they couldn't prove
it. Whatever happened to him?"

"That's that nigga right there!" Irk exclaimed.

"Well, I'll be damn!" Zo replied, astonished.

Irk found a parking spot, cut the engine and stepped
out of the car with Zo right behind him. They walked back
up the block side by side. Zo had his right hand wrapped
around one of his guns as they proceeded towards Henry.

Henry was in the process of putting his duffel bag of
clothes into his truck when he spotted the dark blue Benz
drive slowly past him. If it weren't for the fact that the car
was tricked out, he wouldn't have paid it any mind. But
as it drove slowly down the block then turned, his senses
told him to watch his back. Something didn't feel right.
He'd been in plenty of situations to know when to listen
to his gut, and this was one of them.

He placed the bag in the back of his truck, then closed
the door. When he looked back up the block, he saw two
guys walking slowly towards him. One had his hand
inside of his jacket, while the other one was staring in his
direction. Henry felt for his piece and flipped the safety
off in order to be ready for whatever. He stood behind his
truck, keeping a barrier between them and himself just in
case they were up to no good. As the two figures got closer,
Henry tried to see if he knew them. He didn't recognize
them, so he stayed on his guard.

When Irk and Zo were close enough, Irk cleared his
throat, and in an aggressive tone asked, "Hey, part-na! I
need to holla at'cha!" Zo stayed behind Irk, ready for the
drama if Henry decided to be uncooperative.

Henry stepped to the side just enough to be seen,
then replied in a calm voice, "I don't think I'm who you're
looking for, son!"

"Son! Son! Listen, I'm not your son, nor am I here for

a social visit, nigga! I heard you're looking to open shop on my blocks. You know, move a little work and try to eat from the same plate that I'm eating from already."

Henry was confused at first, then realized that homeboy was trying to check him about the proper etiquette of going through the proper channels in order to sell in someone else's spot. Well, he didn't have the time or the patience to sit here and make friends, so he decided to cut him short and deal with his ass later. "Yeah, yeah, yeah. I hear ya, but check it. Since I'm on the move right now, I'ma holla at 'cha later about that, a'ight?" He was about to step from behind his truck, until he noticed the look on Irk's face. He quietly pulled out his burner from behind him and held it low so they couldn't see it. If it came to that, he wanted to be ready with the first blow.

"I don't give a fuck what you gots to do, nigga! I'm talking to your monkey ass now! See, not only did you disrespect me with that shit, you also tried to make a move on my girl too. Who do you think you are fucking with, nigga?" Irk shouted just loud enough to get his point across.

Henry didn't like his tone, and he let it be known. "Hey! First of all, I don't know what the fuck you're talking about. Who the fuck is your girl anyway?"

"Oh! Oh! Oh! Look, Zo! This nigga wants to play stupid! Well, let me refresh your memory. Her name is Myah. You saw her at the mall earlier. Ring a bell?"

"Nah, duke. Like I said before, I don't think I'm the one you're looking for."

Now Irk was starting to get pissed, and Zo knew it by the way he was standing and sounding. He stepped closer towards Irk and the truck, which caused Henry to get defensive.

"Whoa! Whoa! Whoa, nigga!" Henry pulled his gun up and pointed it at Zo, who stopped in his tracks, realizing that ole boy had the drop on him. "Don't be Captain Save-a-Nigga and get yourself dropped out here, duke!" Henry said as he motioned for Zo to drop his piece. "Lift that shirt up slowly!"

Zo did as he was told and dropped his two guns on the sidewalk. Henry then told Irk to do the same. Irk hesitated, since he couldn't believe that this nigga was doing this.

Henry looked around to make sure no one was around before he did what he was about to do. He slowly made his way around the truck, and walked straight up to Irk and hit him over the head with the butt of the gun he held in his hand, causing Irk to fall over, grasping at the open wound on the side of his forehead.

Zo was about to rush Henry, but thought twice about it when Henry turned the pistol on him. "Nigga, you don't come down here telling me a damn thang! This is supposed to be your bodyguard or something?" Henry asked as he kept the barrel of the gun trained on Zo's chest. Henry's adrenaline was pumping. All of this brought back old memories of his heydays before getting locked up. Even though he was talking to Irk, his eyes stayed on Zo. He was too big for Henry to just overlook him. He didn't want him to get any ideas of being a hero. "Now, take y'all asses outta here before I change my mind about what I really wanna do!" Henry said in a serious voice.

Zo helped Irk to his feet and took him back down the block from which they had come. When they were a good distance away, Irk yelled back, "This ain't over, nigga! It ain't over!"

Henry smiled, waited until they dipped around the corner, hopped into his truck and drove slowly down the block. When he turned the corner, he spotted Irk and Zo getting into the blue Benz he saw earlier. He held his gun out of the driver's side window, and as he drove past he fired three quick shots into the open door of the vehicle, then sped off. "Now, it's over!" he said as he continued on towards the Thruway, heading north towards Upstate.

NINETEEN

While Henry made his way onto the Thruway heading north, Irk was on his way to the hospital, fighting for his life. One of the three shots that Henry let off as he drove past hit Irk in the chest, which collapsed his right lung. Zo, who was hit in the back, was able to call 911 before he passed out.

The neighborhood was once again swarming with uniformed police, collecting evidence and canvassing the block, going door to door, hoping to find someone — anyone — that might have heard or saw anything that could help them find the shooter.

Neither victim was able to talk before they were rushed off to the hospital, which made the investigation that much more difficult.

"I can't believe this!" a plain-clothed detective said out loud as he walked towards the dark blue Benz that was being dusted for fingerprints. "Isn't this the same block that Detective Williamson was murdered on?" he asked a uniformed officer.

"Yeah, it's like déjà vu," the officer replied in a low voice.

"Get this! One of the victims is Dirk Wright, the kingpin of the Bronx!"

"Wow! I wonder what he was doing around here, the detective shot back.

"It looks like someone did a drive-by as they were getting in the car. Both victims were hit from this direction." The officer motioned towards the street.

"Oh, wait a minute!"

The detective's radio crackled, and the news of Dirk's fate came over the radio. "Yeah, one of the victims died before they were able to reach the hospital."

The detective grabbed his radio from off his side and pressed the button to talk. "This is Detective Clark. I'm on the scene. Can you tell me which one of the victims was pronounced DOA (Dead on Arrival)? Over!"

After a couple of seconds, the voice came back. "Ah, yeah, detective. It was Dirk Wright. He died from a gunshot wound to the chest."

"Copy that. How's the other victim? Over!"

"He's gonna make it. He's in surgery right now."

"Is he coherent?" Over!"

"Neg-a-tive!"

Clark now had a murder on his hands that he needed to solve quickly. He placed his radio back on his side, then motioned for the officer with him that he was leaving. Once he was back at his unmarked car, he surveyed the scene once more before hopping inside to head to the hospital to talk to the surviving victim.

Myah, who was on the phone with Nikki, was unaware of what was going on with Irk, as she told her best friend of who was coming to visit her. "Yeah, he said he had something to tell me, but couldn't talk over the phone about it."

"Is that the guy with the dreads that came over to you at the party in the club before we left?" Nikki asked, trying to picture who Myah was talking about.

"Yeah, that's him. He's on his way up right now. Matter of fact, let me call Irk to let him know I made it alright. You know how my baby worries about me." Myah laughed out loud as she remembered how Irk sounded over the phone when he called her last.

"Well, I'm coming over there," Nikki said in an authoritative voice.

"Damn, girl! You sound as if you're my man or something. Didn't we talk about this before?"

"I was just playing, Myah. Besides, I could be, if you ever decide to leave them alone."

They both laughed, then Myah decided to get off of the phone so that she could get herself ready before Tony got there. Before she said good-bye, Nikki quickly added, "Maybe I could come over and keep him company. He was kinda cute at the club that night. Who knows? He might be the one that could turn me back to dick!"

Myah knew that her friend was just joking, but she played it off as if she didn't. "Gir-r-r-l, you better keep your hot ass in Canton, unless you want your feelings hurt!"

Nikki was shocked by the aggressive tone that Myah had said that with, and didn't know how to take it. "Ummm, I… I was just…"

Myah cut her off with a loud outburst, then said, "I knew I would get you! Girl, I'll talk to you later, a'ight?"

"That wasn't funny, Myah!"

"Yes it was! Bye-e-e-!" With that, Myah clicked off the phone, laughing to herself.

Detective Clark arrived at Bronx Memorial Hospital, only to find a slew of people crowding the emergency room. "Excuse me! Excuse me!" he shouted as he made his way through the impatient crowd.

A young man who was waiting at the nurse's station turned around once he heard the well-dressed detective shouting, and said, "There's a line, Mister!"

Clark pulled out his badge and held it up to the tall man's face to show him that he didn't have to wait in any line. The young man stepped to the side to let the detective by, and mumbled under his breath, "Damn pig!" Even though Clark heard him, he continued on, not wanting to cause a scene.

The lady behind the nurse's station looked up from her computer and asked, "May I help you, sir?"

"Yes. I'm here to see a victim that just came in with a gunshot wound to the back."

The older looking white nurse typed something on the computer, then without looking up, said, "He's in room 237. He just came out of surgery."

The detective thanked here and proceeded down the corridor, and headed to the stairs.

Zo was in the ICU (Intensive Care Unit), heavily sedated. The bullet had just missed his spine, and he was laid up with tubes everywhere. A uniformed officer was in the room with him when Clark entered. "How is he?" Clark asked.

"Ah, he'll make it. The doctor said he should be fine."

"Has he said anything yet?" Detective Clark asked as he took off his suit jacket and placed it on a nearby chair.

"Nah. He just came out of surgery. He's doped up pretty good."

"I see." Clark walked over towards the bed and looked down at the patient as he slept. "I hope he can give us something to go on."

"He probably didn't even see who shot him, since his back was turned," the officer stated.

"Let's hope he did," Clark added.

Just as the detective was about to sit down in one of the two chairs facing the patient, a man in his late forties, with a long white jacket walked into the room with his head down as he read a chart. He looked up when he heard Clark's voice. "Oh, I didn't know anyone was in here besides the officer. "I'm Doctor Devin Bice. And you are?" Dr. Bice held out his hand for Clark to take it, which he did.

"I'm Detective Clark, from the 43rd Precinct. I was hoping to get some information from your patient, if at all possible." Clark, who was a little taller than the doctor, stepped back to give him some room.

"Well, I'm afraid that's not going to happen for some time, considering he's heavily sedated. He should come around in about a day or so. As you know, he's lost a lot of blood. We almost lost him, but he's a fighter, I'll give him that," Dr. Bice said as he checked the intravenous bag to make sure that it was dripping properly.

Detective Clark grabbed his suit jacket, pulled out a business card from his inside pocket, and handed it to the doctor. "Well, when he does come around, will you please give me a call? My office and home numbers are on this. I will surely appreciate it."

The doctor took the card, looked at it, then said, "I'll

make sure you are the first one."

With that said, Detective Clark and the young officer stepped out of the room and headed for the stairs, leaving the doctor with his patient.

Once they were gone, Dr. Bice went over to Zo and looked at him for a second, before heading out himself. As he turned, he didn't notice that Zo was trying to open his eyes, which felt like two lead weights. He moved his right hand to show that he was indeed awake, but it was too late, as he listened to the door close shut.

Tony was just entering Watertown, which was about an hour and a half away from the town of Potsdam. He pulled into a gas station that sat right off the main road. "Damn! All these towns up here have one thing in common. They all have a Main Street," he said to himself as he pulled up to a self-service pump to fill his gas tank. He cut the engine off, got out and walked towards the glass enclosure to find the clerk to pay for his gas. While inside, he found something to snack on and to drink.

"Will that be all, Mister?" the young white attendant asked.

Tony pulled out his wallet and said, "Yeah. Can you put twenty on pump number two for me?"

The clerk punched in the amount on the computer and added up the items that Tony placed on the counter. "That'll be twenty-seven eighty-five."

Tony gave him a twenty and a ten-dollar bill, and told him to keep the change. After he gathered his bag to leave, he looked at his watch and figured that he should call Myah now and tell her where he was. He made good time, since traffic was a little bit of nothing. He pulled out his cell phone while he waited for the gas tank to top off, and punched in her number. It rang three times before she answered it.

"Hello-o-o-o!"

"Hey! I'm about an hour and a half away," he said into the phone.

Myah looked at her watch and saw that it was going on six-twenty. "So, you should be here around eight o'clock, huh?"

Tony looked at his watch and figured that was about right. "Yeah, give or take a few minutes."

"Well, I'll be waiting for you. Remember, Lawrence Hall, room 215."

Tony smiled as he put the gas nozzle back in its cradle. "I'll remember. Bye!"

After they hung up, Tony got into his car and pulled back out onto the main street, and followed the directions that his GPS had given him in order to head in the right direction towards Potsdam.

Henry drove over the Tappan Zee Bridge and headed north, passing Westchester on his way towards New Rochelle. His system was bumping the Lox's new CD, which kept him pumped up as the traffic moved along at a steady pace. Once he made it onto the Thruway, he knew that he'd be able to cruise without having to brake. He had plenty of gas and money, so he wasn't worried about a thing.

His main concern was finding Myah. He didn't know exactly where she would be, but he knew that everyone in college partied hard, especially on the weekends, so all he had to do was head to one of the local clubs and wait;

wait either for her to show up, or for someone that knew her. He had a recent picture of her, so all he had to do was show it to a couple of guys around the club, and he was bound to hit pay dirt.

He was determined to find her and give her what she's been waiting for so long; the chance to get even. But it wasn't going to be that easy. He knew that she would deny him, so he was prepared to take what she fought so hard to keep away from him.

"Yeah, bitch! I'm getting that ass tonight!" He was getting hard just thinking about how she would fight, just like her mother did twelve years ago. So, as he approached the Thruway that would take him to Potsdam, New York, he sang along with the music that was playing throughout the truck:

> *"...Ride or Die,*
> *You want it, we got it,*
> *We live it!*
> *Ride or Die..."*

TWENTY

Ever since they found out that Detective Williamson was gunned down outside of the Terrance Avenue Apartments, Moody and Stevens, who were both working unofficially with the detective on the Anderson case, backed off. But they were both kept informed of what was going on through some of their contacts within the department. It was too much of a coincidence that right before Williamson was about to leave the area, someone just happened to shoot him dead, let alone the fact that he was watching a known killer that tried to kill cops before. Something just didn't add up, and they wanted to find out whether their hunches were true.

Stevens dug a little deeper into Henry's past, and found out that Myah had been writing to him for about three years. He learned through Elmira's mailroom personnel that Henry received letters, pictures, and even money orders from a Ms. Myah Johnson while he was in their custody. She even went to visit him in Danamora while he was there before he was released.

Stevens relayed the information to Moody, who in turn informed him that Henry's baby's mother, Libretta

Nichols, was found in a hotel room with her throat cut. They both agreed that Henry was behind that incident, but after Detective Williamson was found dead in his car just up the street from where Henry lived, it made them realize that their suspicions were true all along.

They had to contact Myah, and hope that she could tell them her reason for getting involved with the one suspect that was linked to her mother's death, even after knowing of his violent background.

Moody decided that they needed to find her fast if they were to find Henry. His gut feelings were telling him that she might be his next victim if he found out exactly who she was. Or, was that her intention all along?

"Mr. Wright was pronounced dead before he reached us," Dr. Bice said sullenly as he stood next to Zo's bed.

The only words Zo could say were, "No! No! No-o-o-o!" The first thing that he asked once he was fully awake was if Irk was alright.

Dr. Bice didn't want to be the bearer of bad news, but he wasn't going to lie either.

Zo tried to turn over, but couldn't because of the tubes that were still in his arm and nose, so he just laid there with tears in his eyes, and a blank expression on his face. The pain in his back brought back the realization that he was seriously hurting, but the news of Irk's death was just too much for him to bear. Anger replaced the feeling of sadness, and now he wanted nothing more than to kill the muthafucka that took away his best friend. "I need to talk to the police, right now!" he yelled to Dr. Bice once the tears were gone.

"There was this detective that wanted to talk to you

once you were able to talk. I gave him a call before I came in to see you. Now, calm down and let me check your dressings," Dr. Bice said in a soft voice, hoping to calm his patient down a little. He did a few check ups of the dressing on the wound, then left after receiving a page from the front desk.

When he returned, Detective Clark was with him, along with a uniformed officer that stood at the door like a bodyguard, while the detective approached the bed to talk to Zo about the incident that left his best friend dead, and him in ICU.

Tony made it to Myah's dorm at about eight o'clock. He parked his car in one of the parking spaces that was reserved for visitors, got out and walked up the concrete steps that led to the front door of Lawrence Hall. The first thing that caught his attention was how nice the campus was. The grounds were immaculately kept, and the buildings looked as if they were built just a few months ago.

As he made his way through the front door, he entered the lobby, where a few girls were hanging around talking. When they saw him looking around as if he were lost, one of the four girls walked towards him and asked, "Can I help you, sir?"

Tony was caught off guard. He looked down and saw a beautiful young girl that looked to be about eighteen, with long straight black hair, brown eyes and the smile of an angel. She was dressed in a pullover sweater and a pair of blue jeans that hugged her small frame nicely. He smiled and said, "Nah, I'm cool. Your school is beautiful!"

The young girl smiled, then said, "Thank you!" as if she was the reason why. She rejoined her girlfriends, and as Tony made his way towards the stairway to take him up to the second floor, the girls followed him with their eyes, commenting the whole time at how fine he looked.

"Did you see his eyes? Oh my God, he's so fine!" one of the girls said as she held her hands in front of her mouth.

All of them agreed, and wondered whom the lucky girl was that he came to see.

Myah was sitting at her desk, reading the latest issue of *Vibe* magazine, when a knock at the door startled her. She jumped up, closed the magazine, and walked over towards the door as she threw the book on her bed. "Who is it?" she asked while she looked at herself in the full-length mirror that was hung behind the door.

"It's Tony!"

Myah looked at her watch, which read eight-seventeen, and yelled back, "It's about time!" and opened the door to let him in.

Tony stood in the doorway, looking as if he was lost. Myah smiled, and then motioned for him to come inside. Once he was fully in, she closed the door and walked over to her desk. "Have a seat," she told him while giving him the once-over.

He was wearing a blue and plaid Marc Echo pullover shirt, with baggy blue Dockers pants, and a pair of navy blue Marc Echo boots. His dreads were hanging loosely, which came to about his shoulders. He was also sporting a twenty-four inch Rolex chain with a diamond encrusted cross that hung to the middle of his chest. Myah's first impression of him was that he was definitely a good looking brother. She could see why her mother had fallen for him.

As Tony took a seat on Myah's bed, he continued to survey her room. "So, this is what a girl's dorm room looks like, huh?" he asked, not really expecting an answer.

"I know you didn't drive eight hours just to see what my room looks like, so, what's up?" She wasn't trying to be rude, but she wanted to know what was so important that would make him drive all the way there in order to tell her.

When he finally settled his eyes on her, he was taken aback a little. She looked so much like her mother that it brought back some memories that he had from a long time ago. Myah was wearing a honey colored Baby Phat two-piece, with the pants fitting her thick body like a glove. She had her long black hair cascading over the right side of her face, which made her look so innocent. Under her shirt she wore a white tank top that went well with her white Nike AirMax sneakers. Her body was accented nicely by the outfit she was wearing, which wasn't lost on Tony. He looked away, hoping she didn't catch him staring too long at her thick frame. "Damn! Can't a friend just want to visit once in a while?" he said jokingly.

Henry was now four hours away from the town of Potsdam, where he knew he would find Myah. Since he didn't have a clue as to where her school was, or even the room she stayed in, he did know that he would eventually find someone who did.

He thought about what he wanted to do to her, which made him smile as he drove past the Glenn Falls exit. "I'ma make that bitch scream so bad!" he said out loud. His mind continued to think of different things that should have warned him of what she was trying to do. "That bitch is smart as a muthafucka! She really had me going!"

Henry looked at the next exit that was coming up, and realized that his GPS was telling him to take the next left. "This muthafucka is so-o-o-o dope!" he said as he took the next left and headed towards Tupper Lake.

"Bitch, you're mine!"

As Nikki sat on her bed with her phone next to her, she wondered what Myah was doing. She knew that Tony was coming up, which was the reason why she was so anxious to find out what they were talking about. She thought about calling, but then again, she didn't want Myah to get mad if she was interrupting her. Then she thought about just driving over there and showing up unexpectedly. She was beside herself, and as she looked at her clock on the wall, it read nine-twenty-one.

She decided to give Myah a call to let her know she was going out to BackStreets, just in case she wanted to reach her.

She dialed Myah's number, and as she waited for her to answer, thoughts ran through her head of Myah and Tony fucking. The phone rang three times before she answered,

"Hello!"

"Hey, girl! I know you're busy, but I just wanted to let you know that I was heading down to BackStreets. I have to get out of this dorm."

Myah smiled and waved for Tony to hold on. "You know what? I think I'm gonna go too. I'll bring Tony down there to let him see how we party. I'll meet you there, okay?"

"What time are you leaving?" Nikki asked, smiling.

"We'll leave around ten."

"I'll meet y'all at the bar, okay?"

"A'ight, girl. Don't drink too much. You know how you get! Myah said jokingly.

"Oh, shut up!" Nikki replied, laughing. "What did Tony have to tell you?"

Myah lowered her voice in order for Tony not to hear, and said, "I'll tell you later."

Nikki knew that Myah probably couldn't talk at that moment, so she didn't press the issue. "Oh, okay. I'll see you soon then."

When Nikki hung up, she got dressed and headed down to BackStreets to wait for Myah.

Tony told everything he knew, and even what he thought he knew, concerning Henry.

Myah never let on that she knew Henry personally. She just listened, letting him say what he had to say. As he talked, she knew that she had to do something soon before it backfired on her. She wanted to get even with Henry for what he did, but she still was undecided as to how she was going to go about it. She thought of telling Tony about her dealings with Henry and what she planned to do, but thought better of it after he told her about his theories. Nevertheless, she had to come up with a plan that would either put Henry back in prison, or kill him for taking her mother from her.

Little did Myah know, Henry was planning to confront her and expose her little plan of revenge. As she and Tony got ready to head to BackStreets, he was now only two hours from Potsdam. He would ultimately spoil her plans... and possibly her life!

TWENTY-ONE

"Are you sure?"

"Hell yeah! I know who the fuck shot me. If I wasn't laid up in this fuckin' bed right now, I wouldn't need y'all's asses! I would take care of it myself! That muthafucka killed my man! I want his ass probably more than y'all do!" Zo stated to Detective Clark as he gave his statement.

Detective Clark got on his two-way radio and barked orders to dispatch. "I want an APB (All Points Bulletin) on a 2000 white Lincoln Navigator! Suspect's name is Hendrick S. Anderson. I repeat! Hendrick S. Anderson. Suspect is armed and dangerous! Be advised, he is armed and dangerous!"

The dispatcher typed in the information on her computer, then got on the airways to inform all units to be on the lookout.

Once everyone had left, Zo laid in his bed and thought about everything that went down. As he closed his eyes, a tear ran down his face. He thought about Irk, and how a good friend was taken before his time.

Then, he thought about how Myah would take it. "Oh shit! I gotta tell her before someone else does!" he said as he tried to get out of bed. But the pain in his back was just to much for him to bear, so he laid back down. He would have to wait until he was able to move again before he could even attempt to tell Myah anything.

He also felt bad about talking to the cops, but he knew that was the only way he felt that he could catch the muthafucka that did this. He knew that once he was caught, he could find a way to get street justice, even if he was behind bars. All Zo had to do was wait for the cops to pick his black ass up. He knew that news traveled fast, so it wouldn't take long before he could find a way to get him.

Nikki arrived at the bar at around ten-fifteen. As usual, the place was packed with college students from both Potsdam and Clarkson Universities. There were a few that came from Canton Community College, which was ten miles away, but the majority of the crowd was local.

As she waited in line to gain admittance, she looked around to see whether Myah's car was anywhere around. When she didn't see any sign of it, she then looked inside the club's picture window that took up most of the front. She saw no signs of her or Tony anywhere.

"Next two!" the burly looking bouncer shouted from the door after letting two club goers out.

Nikki stepped through the front door, paid her two dollar fee, and was immediately hit by the heat that was coming from inside. The weather outside was just cool enough to wear a light jacket without freezing, but once inside, the temperature went up about thirty degrees because of all of the body heat.

Nikki was wearing a pair of Baby Phat low rider jeans, with a cream colored blouse. Her hair was done up in Shirley Temple curls, with highlights that brought out her green eyes. She was looking cute, which she knew.

She made her way over to the bar and found a chair to sit on. The bartender came to her, and she ordered a diet Coke. When he left, she turned around to look at the crowded dance floor, hoping to see someone she knew. She looked at her watch and saw that it was now 10:45. "Damn! Where is she?" she questioned.

The bartender placed her drink on the bar in front of her, and she slid him the money she had in her hand, then said with a smile, "Thank you!" loud enough for him to hear over the loud music that the DJ was playing.

"Ayo, look!" Jayson shouted to his man, Capone as they looked at Nikki at the bar, sipping on her drink. "Yo, kid, that's a bad ass snowflake over there! I wouldn't mind banging that tonight! She looks like she would be a freak in bed," Jayson said while grabbing his crotch to emphasize his point.

"That bitch ain't gonna fuck with your ass, nigga! I have a better chance of bagging that piece than you do. Matter of fact, hold this!" Capone handed his man his Heineken, then walked over towards the bar, leaving Jayson at the pool table, wondering what he was going to do.

Capone slowly approached Nikki from the right side as she was just about to turn around to face the bar. "Hey, boo! What school you go to?" he asked as he sat in the empty seat next to her.

At first, Nikki didn't know if he was talking to her or someone else. She turned to face him, and was shocked to see that he was half-ass good looking. She smiled when she realized that he was talking to her. "Excuse me?" she asked with an attitude.

"I said, what school you go to? I haven't seen you in here before, because if I had, I would have made it my business to know who you were."

Nikki liked his talk game. He was definitely a slick talker. She also knew that guys would say anything just to get in a girl's pants, but instead of blowing him off like she usually did, she decided to see what he was about. Besides, she had nothing better to do. When she sees Myah and Tony walk in, she would excuse herself, she thought.

But, Capone had other plans on his mind for her.

Tony parked his car a couple of blocks from the club, since the streets were lined with students' cars. He and Myah hopped out, and walked to the club amongst a few others that were also headed in that direction.

Myah wanted to show Tony a good time, since it was his first time up at her school. They both were dressed casual, with Myah wearing a pair of tan Gap jeans with a matching jacket, and a white tank top shirt.

As they approached the line at the front door of the club, Tony let out an exasperated sigh.

"Don't worry, the line goes quick," Myah said to ease his frustration.

"So it's not like in the city, huh?"

"No! There's always someone coming out, so it moves."

Tony saw the line moving, so he relaxed a little, not wanting Myah to see his anxiousness. He still had on what he drove there in. He just wanted to get in, get something to drink, and unwind, especially after the long ride up.

Once they were inside, Myah looked around for Nikki, who said she would be waiting at the bar, but as

Myah made her way to the bar, she saw no signs of her anywhere. She scanned the dance floor and saw someone that appeared to look like Nikki, all hugged up with some guy in the back near the speakers. Myah told Tony that she would be right back, and for him to wait by the bar. She quickly made a beeline for the dance floor to see if that was, in fact, Nikki.

Nikki's head was spinning, and everything seemed a blur. It was hard for her to focus or breathe. She needed some air.

Capone saw the obvious signs that Nikki was displaying someone being drunk, so he quickly asked whether she was alright. "Hey, boo, you a'ight?"

Nikki looked at him, but couldn't remember his name. "Ahh, yeah-h-h, I think so," was all she could say as she slipped into semi-unconsciousness.

Capone grabbed her around her waist, wrapped his arm around her as if they were walking out, and led her to the front door and out into the parking lot where he had his car parked. His plan was to take her to his apartment and have his way with her. He knew that the Visine drops that he put into her drink would only last a couple of hours at the most, so he wanted to have as much fun with her as he could. "I'm gonna fuck the shit out of you, bitch!" he said in a low voice as he dragged her towards his car.

Stevens and Moody heard about the APB that was put out for Henry, and knew exactly where he might be heading after learning that he was last seen going towards the Thruway. Stevens tried several times to call Myah's dorm room, but when he realized that she wasn't there, he decided to alert the authorities up in Potsdam of the situation.

Henry was now only twenty minutes away from Potsdam, so he decided to stay low key by driving only on the back roads in order to not raise any suspicions or draw unwanted attention to his tricked out truck.

Once he entered the town of Potsdam, he made his way down Main Street, where all of the bars were located. Even though he had no clue as to where Myah might be, he knew that if he asked enough people, somebody was bound to lead him to her whereabouts.

He parked his truck in a parking lot of one of the clubs. The sign out front read BackStreets, and there were people out front still trying to get in. "This looks like a good place to start," he said to himself as he turned off the engine and stepped out with Myah's picture in his right hand.

As he made his way towards the front, he thought he saw something between two of the cars that were situated in the back where he had parked his truck. He walked over to get a closer look, and saw a young black male struggling to get what looked to be like a cute little snow bunny inside of a car. She was obviously too drunk to stand on her own. When the two made eye contact, Henry smiled and said, "Handle your business, my nigga!"

The stunned young brother smiled back and replied, "You know I am!"

Henry walked on around the corner, and straight to the front door of BackStreets in order to get the bouncer to let him in, even though there were people in line waiting to get in.

Once Henry had disappeared around the corner of Backstreet, Capone managed to get Nikki's body in the backseat of his roommate's silver four door Chevy Malibu.

He had convinced him that he was only using it to go to the club and back and in return, he would fill his gas tank up since his roommate was running low on cash. With the thought of free gas, his roommate didn't hesitate to hand over the keys.

Now here Capone was struggling to put a girl's body inside the back seat in order to take her back to his dorm room.

After realizing just how hard it was to move dead weight around, Capone decided to just take care of business right there in the parking lot. His dick was rock hard as he looked at Nikki's thick thighs through her tight Baby Phat low rider jeans. The light color blouse that she was wearing was barely able to hide the swells of her firm, perky tits that Capone slowly massaged as he unbuttoned her shirt. He was enjoying himself and the look on face showed it.

Just as he was about to unbutton her jeans, Nikki moved her head as if she was trying to shake off the effects of the visine, but when she stopped, he continued to unbutton her pants, this time with a little more urgency than he had before.

The last thing he wanted was for her to wake up and scream rape. He didn't know what he would do if she did, but he did know he wasn't going back to jail for nothing or no one.

When he was finally able to slip a leg out of her tight fitted jeans, he couldn't hold out any longer. As he stared at her clean shaven pussy, he fumbled in the front of his jeans, found what he was looking for and ripped opened the package. He placed the condom on his dick, which was sticking straight in front of him like a steal pole, and proceeded to roll it as far down as he could.

Once he was sure it was on tight enough, Capone placed his hands between Nikki's thighs and began to spread them apart in order to get inside of her.

Since she wasn't wet enough to penetrate, he put two fingers inside of her and moved them around hoping that the stimulation would bring forth lubrication. Which after two minutes of doing so, Capone was rewarded with some wetness. It was just enough he needed in order to enter her.

"AAhh!" was all that he could manage to say as he slowly thrusted himself in and out of her pussy, which only seemed to get wetter with each stroke. The feeling was like a velvet glove that enveloped his dick. The tightness along with the wetness brought Capone to that point of no return.

"Ohhh! Ohhh! Ohhh! Yeahhh!!!" he moaned excitedly as he tried to hold back, but couldn't. He let loose what felt like a truck load of cum inside of her. Luckily, he was wearing a condom, which caught every drop of his seed. He knew that if he didn't have one on, he would have definitely came inside of her with no thoughts of the consequences.

"Damn! If your pussy is this good with a condom on, I can imagine what it'll feel like without one, and you weren't even into it. Damn! That's some good ass pussy. I wasn't even in it a minute before it had me cumming." Capone was contemplating about going at it again, but decided not to as he slipped out of Nikki's pussy in order to take off the cum filled condom.

Being careful as not to lose it inside of her, Capone slowly backed away while at the same time holding the base of the condom with his right thumb and index finger.

He was about to set Nikki's up in order to dress her, but after a couple of attempts to do so, he got frustrated and abandoned that idea. He looked at his watch and saw that he's been fucking around with her for almost an hour. He then realized that the club was about to close, which would flood the parking lot with kids trying to get back to the dorms.

Scared that someone might see him, he opened the back door, looking around to make sure no one was around, then pushed Nikki's body out onto the asphalt with her jeans and panties around one leg and her shirt completely off of her.

Capone then started the car and pulled out of the parking lot without even looking back, leaving Nikki's body laying there for all to see.

While Henry was trying to convince the bouncer out front to let him in, Myah approached the young couple that were making out in the back of the club. When she got a little closer, she realized that it wasn't Nikki at all. The couple looked up from what they were doing, and gave her a cold stare, as if to say, "What tha fuck!"

Myah turned back around and headed back to the bar to join Tony, who had ordered them two drinks. "Did you find your friend?" Tony asked as Myah sat down next to him.

"No! She should have been here by now."

'I'm sure she's coming. She's probably running late. Why don't you call her?"

Myah felt for her phone, then realized that she had left it in her room. "Ah, damn it! I left it back in my room.

You have yours on you?" she asked him while he took a sip of his rum and Coke.

Tony reached inside of his leather jacket with his right hand and pulled out his cell phone and handed it to her. She flipped it open, dialed Nikki's cell phone number, then waited for her to answer. When her voice mail picked up, Myah ended the call. She then tried Nikki's dorm room, hoping that she was there. The result was the same. "Damn!" she yelled as she flipped Tony's cell closed, holding it in her left hand as she thought about where Nikki might be.

As soon as Henry entered the bar, the heat was the first thing that he noticed. "Got damn!" he said as he made his way through the crowd of people that were either coming in or going out.

With Myah's picture in hand, he looked around to see if he could find someone to ask about her. He saw a tall dark skinned young brother that looked to be somewhat normal, compared to all the country bumpkins he saw since he walked in. "Ayo!" he yelled, hoping to get his attention.

The brother looked up from his conversation with a pretty white girl, and started to walk over towards Henry. Once he was close enough, Henry asked him if he ever saw Myah, as he showed him her picture. The young brother shook his head to say no, then said, "I wish I did! She's fine as hell! That's you, son?" he asked Henry.

The look on Henry's face immediately told the young brother to keep it moving. When he thanked him, the young brother walked back over to the white girl he was talking to earlier, and continued with his conversation as if he never missed a beat.

Henry scanned the dance floor, then the bar. When he saw Myah at the bar with some Dread, he quickly played the shadows in order not to be seen. As he watched from the corner trying to observe her every move, Myah couldn't enjoy herself because of how worried she was for Nikki.

"Hey, Tony, let's finish these drinks so that we can get out of here. I'm worried about Nikki. It's not like her to tell me she'll be someplace and not show up."

Tony looked at his watch, then turned towards the dance floor to scan the area. The place was like hook-up central, where every guy was either trying or succeeding in finding someone for the night. Just as he was about to turn back around, a boy around Myah's age came between him and her without even asking whether they were together. He just started conversing with her as if Tony wasn't even there.

"Hey, girl. Damn, you're fine-e-e-e! Can a brother get some play or what?"

Myah looked at him as if he was repulsive and said, "Nigga, please! I ain't got the time nor the energy to even respond to your corny ass! Go away!"

The brother was about to say something disrespectful, but before he had a chance to, Tony cleared his throat and said in a calm but loud enough voice to be heard over the music, "She's with me."

The young brother turned around and realized that Tony looked too intimidating for him to blow off, so he basically licked his wounds and moved on. "A'ight! A'ight! My bad!" was all he could say as he walked towards a group of guys that were watching him get rejected.

"Okay, are you ready?" Tony asked Myah after finishing his drink.

Myah got up from her seat and said, "Been ready!"

They walked towards the front door, and as they passed by a dark corner, Myah swore she saw someone that looked like Henry. Before she could get a closer look, Tony placed his arm over her shoulder and led her past a crowd of people that were trying to get in.

Henry watched Myah and her friend leave the club from the dark corner he was standing in. Once they were out the door, he made his way through the crowd of students and through the front door. He looked up and down the street to see which way they went, and after his eyes adjusted, he spotted them turning the corner. He quickly went to the parking lot that he left his truck in, and passed by the young white girl that was with the young brother he saw earlier. She was between two cars, passed out with her pants around her ankles, exposing her clean-shaven pussy for all to see. Henry thought about helping her, but then thought better of it.

He hopped into his truck and started the engine. He pulled out of his spot and drove slowly past the young girl again, this time stopping in front of her. He got his look on, as she laid on her back. *She's cute even when she's sleeping,* he thought to himself. He saw some people coming his way, so he put his truck into drive and drove towards the street, and made a right onto Main Street.

Tony and Myah drove towards the Clarkson campus so she could get her car. Tony was feeling beat from the long drive up, so he decided to call it a night. Myah showed him the hotel that people stayed in when they came to visit. *I'll drop her off, then check in,* he thought to himself as they entered the parking lot of her dorm.

Little did he know, they were being followed the whole time.

As Nikki lay unconscious between two cars in the parking lot of BackStreets, a group of Potsdam students — two girls and three boys who were heading to their cars after a night of club hopping and drinking — spotted her as they walked by. "Oh my God!" one of the girls screamed as she covered her mouth in disbelief.

"Damn!" was all the guys could say as they saw the pretty blond headed girl lying on her back with her jeans and panties around one ankle and her legs spread apart. She was obviously sexually assaulted by the way she was positioned.

"Someone call the police!" the taller girl said as she went over to Nikki to see if she was alright.

"Wake up, girl! Wake up!" the shorter one yelled into Nikki's ear as she gently tapped her face to wake her up. Even though she didn't smell alcohol on her, the young girl assumed she was either drunk or high.

As Nikki started coming too, a small crowd had started to gather. One of the girls tried to shoo the boys away who were just there to gawk at the naked girl. Everyone was curious as to how she got that way.

When the police arrived, Nikki was fully awake and curled up with her knees against her chest and tears streaming down her face. She was so disoriented from whatever was given to her by the young brother that sat next to her, that she couldn't remember anything after she passed out.

"Everybody, back away now!" an officer yelled into the crowd of onlookers.

"What happened?" another asked Nikki once they got the situation under control.

Nikki told him that she couldn't remember. Once it was determined that she was drugged, the officer called for an ambulance in order for her to be taken to the Potsdam-Canton Hospital.

Without her phone, Nikki was unable to call Myah, who was now heading up the stairs that led to her dorm.

Henry parked his truck and waited. When he saw the Dread leaving, he stepped out and proceeded to walk at a fast pace towards Myah's building.

Myah entered the front door, unaware that Henry was right behind her. She went down the corridor and towards the stairs that led to the second floor of her dorm. Her mind was so focused on getting to her room that Henry's presence went unnoticed. Since it was around one in the morning and the students that occupied the dorm were either in their rooms or still out clubbing, the hallways were empty. This wasn't unusual for a Friday night.

Myah reached her room and pulled out her keys. She opened the door and stepped inside. Just as she was about to close the door, Henry rushed towards it and stopped it from closing with his right foot, while at the same time, the phone began to ring. When Myah looked up to see who it was, the shocked expression on her face made Henry smile.

"Hey, baby girl! Surprised to see me?" he asked as he pushed her door open and walked in, causing Myah to take a step or two back.

"Wha... wha... what are you doing here?" she shot back while putting distance between them. The phone rang two more times, and then stopped. Myah never took her eyes off of Henry, as she watched him close the door behind him and lock it.

"What's wrong, Myah? I can't come visit my girl at her school?"

Myah was at a loss for words, but managed to regain her composure. "I never said that! I was just caught off guard, that's all. How long have you been here?" She tried to walk towards the phone, but before she had a chance to, Henry yelled for her to stop.

"Sit your conniving ass down before you make me mad, bitch!"

Myah couldn't believe the way he was talking to her. When she turned around to face him, she saw the gun he had in his right hand pointing straight at her. She did what she was told as tears began to run down her face.

Henry moved towards her with a look of pure hatred in his eyes. When he was directly in front of her, he looked down between her thick thighs and smiled. "Damn! I've been out a minute now, and you still haven't given me that ass of yours yet! Now, is that right?"

Myah just stared at the gun that was now caressing her left thigh, and going further up towards her pussy. She was too scared to even scream. When he put the gun down and started talking, she felt a sense of relief.

"I don't need a gun for you, baby girl. In fact, all I want you to do is relax and listen. Before you start lying to me again, let me tell you what I know, a'ight?"

She nodded her head as she wiped the tears away from her face with the back of her hand.

"You's a smart bitch, I'll give you that! You had me

fooled all the way. I should have listened to my man, Ed-Ski, when he told me something was wrong with you. I didn't put it together until I looked closer at your picture. I knew you looked like someone I knew before. Then, it came to me! Twelve years ago, I met this pretty ass bitch that lived at the Castle Hill Projects. Her name was Sonya Johnson. She was a bad bitch too! Long brown hair, like yours! Smooth skin, like yours! And a body that made a nigga do a double-take, like yours!"

As Henry continued to tell her things about her mother, Myah started to get more and more pissed.

"So there I was, sitting outside her building, waiting for her man to leave. When I saw the punk muthafucka pass my truck, I went up to her apartment and opened the door, which wasn't even locked, and found her in the bed, sleeping. I crawled into the bed, and before she could say a word, I punched the bitch in the face. When she started to scream, I beat her unconscious and fucked the bitch while she was dying. Yeah, I killed the bitch!"

Myah's face turned from scared to angry, and Henry knew that he had gotten to her.

"What I didn't know was that the bitch had a daughter. If I did, I would have killed your ass too!" Henry laughed, then backslapped Myah so hard that blood flew from her mouth. "Bitch, you thought that you could get back for what I did to your bitch as mother, huh?" he shouted in an angry voice.

Tony was now in the parking lot of the hotel, when he realized that Myah still had his phone. Before he turned off the engine, he pulled out of the parking space he was sitting in, and headed back to Myah's in order to retrieve his phone.

As he drove, he thought about Tania and what she might have been thinking since he just up and left. He knew that he should have called her once he was with Myah, but he was too focused on letting Myah know exactly what was on his mind, especially since he knew that Henry was back on the streets. Tony still remembered the day that the police had picked him up because they thought that he had killed her mother. It pained him every time he thought about Sonya. She would always be his first love. It even seemed ironic that the girl that he was now with had a similar name—Tania—Sonya. That made him smile a little.

He parked his car in one of the spaces marked for visitors, and got out. He just hoped that Myah was still there. As he walked up the stairs to the front door, he had an eerie feeling that something just wasn't right.

"You don't have to—" Myah shouted before Henry slapped her again with an open hand.

"*Shut the fuck up, bitch!*" he screamed as he continued to rip her tank top off of her. He was on top of her on the other bed. Myah's breasts popped out, once he freed them from her shirt. He bent down and took one of her nipples into his mouth. His dick was as hard as a rock. "Damn! Now this is what I'm talking about!" he said between sucking and caressing her breasts.

Myah tried to fight, but he was too strong for her. He sat on top of her, looking down. Her ripped tank top was spotted with blood from the cut on her lip. As he stared at her breasts that were now fully exposed, he started to unbuckle her jeans. "I'ma give you what you want, bitch!

Just like I gave it to your mom! She fought too. Like mother, like daughter. I'ma run through the whole family!" Henry stated, laughing.

"Henry, no! Please don't do this!" Myah pleaded with tears running down the sides of her face.

"Oh yeah, I do! Since you wanna play games with the pussy, tease a nigga with it, I'ma show you what happens once all the games are over." He got her pants open, then proceeded to pull them down, along with her black silk panties. Now that he had her exposed, he got up off of her, and told her to take them completely off.

Myah crawled off the bed to take her shoes off, then noticed that Henry's gun was sitting on her desk. She turned her head to see what he was doing, and saw that he was looking directly at her from behind.

"Don't be stupid, bitch! I *want* you to go for it. Do something that'll make me kill ya early," Henry said in a calm voice.

While Tony was rounding the corner for the third floor, he was thinking of what he was going to say to Tania once he did call her. He walked down the hallway, and almost passed Myah's room. He backed up, and was about to knock on the door when he heard voices inside. He listened for a minute, not wanting to disturb anything, until he heard what sounded like sobbing.

Henry smacked Myah once more before he pushed her back onto the bed. He was just about to climb on top of her when he heard something outside the door. Myah heard it also, and once Henry turned his head, she yelled, "Help me-e-e-e-e!"

Henry snapped his head back around, and with one quick motion, punched her square on the jaw, knocking her completely unconscious.

When Tony heard Myah's scream for help, he turned the door handle, which was locked. He stepped back two steps and threw his shoulder into the door and pushed his way inside. What he saw once he looked up almost took his breath away. Myah was lying on her bed with only her tank top on, which was ripped in half, exposing her breasts. She was nude from the waist down, and on the side of her was Henry, who was now on his feet. Myah wasn't moving, and the blood on her tank top caused Tony to spring into action.

"You muthafucka!" Tony screamed as he rushed Henry. He tackled him to the floor, and once he was on top, he proceeded to throw a series of blows to his face.

Henry managed to put one arm up to block the punches, then with brute strength, he flipped Tony over. They both scrambled to their feet and squared off.

While Tony knew how to street fight, Henry was trained in the Martial Arts. Tony lunched towards him, but was blocked and given a hard punch to his chest. He recovered quickly, but the pain was evident. Henry moved in and delivered a combination to Tony's body, causing him to double over. Once he did, Henry knew that it was over. He grabbed a handful of Tony's dreads and held him in place long enough to deliver a knee to his face, breaking his nose instantly.

"Ugghh! Agghh!" Tony screamed as he fell backwards. Blood poured out of his nose and coated his clothes and the floor.

Henry smiled and said, "So, you wanna be Captain-

Save-A-Ho, huh?"

As Tony writhed in pain on the floor, Henry straddled him and proceeded to pound his fist into his face. "You stu-pid muth-a-fucka! You should have kept it mo-ving!" With every syllable, a punch was landed, causing Tony to black out from the sheer pain.

Myah started to wake up. The pain in her jaw was excruciating, but somehow she managed to get past it. When she was able to focus, she saw Henry beating Tony, who was now lying on the floor of her room, unconscious. She looked over to her desk and saw Henry's gun. She reached for it and grabbed it by the handle. Her head was still spinning, but she knew she had to do something. Her finger went to the trigger, and just like Irk had taught her, she made sure that the safety was off. Myah held the gun with both hands, and aimed the barrel at Henry's chest. "*Stop!*" she screamed in a weak voice. "Leave him alone!" she said, this time loud enough for him to hear.

When he realized that she had his gun, he stopped what he was doing and stood up.

"Get away from him!" she shouted as she kept the gun trained on his chest.

"What tha fuck you gonna do, shoot me, bitch?" he asked in a low voice. Once he saw her shake her head as if to clear it, he rushed towards her.

Myah saw him coming, and pulled the trigger. The power of the Glock caused the gun to recoil, but she quickly steadied it again.

The bullet hit Henry in the stomach. Blood instantly soaked the shirt he was wearing. He looked down and couldn't believe that she had shot him. He tried to move again, but this time Myah let off two quick shots simultaneously.

"*Bang! Bang!*"

With that, Henry fell to the floor.

The police, who were already alerted to the disturbance, heard the shots and rushed to where they came from. They moved in once they knew the shooter was secured. They found Tony on the floor, unconscious, and Henry lying in a puddle of blood with three shots to his mid-section.

Myah was sitting with her knees drawn close to her chest, shaking, while the gun lay on the bed next to her.

EPILOGUE

Retired Detectives Moody and Stevens were notified about what had happened up in Postdam, since it was them that had first brought it to the Potsdam Police department's attention.

After visiting Myah at the Potsdam-Canton Hospital that night, Moody and Stevens informed her that Henry was dead and that the young man that was found laying beaten and unconscious was just coming out of surgery. He was in critical, but stable condition. When her aunt and uncle were told of the situation, they took the first plane out to be there for their niece. Myah was also told of Irk's death, which made her loose all control. She had to be heavily sedated in order to calm her down.

Once she was fully awake and able to talk to the authorities, she told them along with Det. Moody and Stevens everything that had lead up to Henry's death. Since no one was there to witness the actual shooting, the DA had to do a thorough investigation, which was classified as a first degree murder.

Myah had to stay a total of four days in the hospital in order to fully recover from her injuries, and while she was there, she learned that her best friend Nikki was also admitted to the hospital. She was still going through a serious of test for being drugged and raped.

Her parents wanted to make sure that their daughter didn't have any sexually transmitted diseases or if the drug that was used to knock her out had any side affects that may have caused permanent damage.

They were so furious with not only the school, but also the club for allowing under aged kids to enter their establishment that they planned on suing, so that what happened to their daughter would not happen to someone else's child.

When Myah and Nikki were released from the hospital, they were told to stay close, since the investigation, into both incidents were still on going. Both girls went back to Long Island to recuperate not only from the physical injuries, but also from the mental trauma they endured.

No charges were filed concerning the death of Henry, but questions were still unanswered as to why this had all happened.

Retired Detectives Moody and Stevens knew the answers, but when they were informed that the District Attorney wasn't going to prosecute, they stayed silent. Both figured that enough damage had been done. In essence, they relished in the fact of knowing that justice, even though it wasn't done the legal way, worked to correct a wrong that should have been corrected many years ago.

A month had passed since that awful night in Potsdam, and as Myah walked around her neighborhood, she reflected on everything that had happened. She dropped out of college and moved back home with her aunt and uncle.

After learning what had happened to Nikki while they were at the same hospital, they became even closer than before.

Myah blamed herself for what happened to Irk. If only she would have told him about Henry and what she was planning to do, he might still be alive today. Henry's death still didn't resolve the feelings she felt for the loss of her mother. In fact, she felt even more pain than before. Not only did Henry kill her mother, he was also responsible for the death of Detective Williamson, and Irk as well.

It was hard for her to attend Irk's funeral, but she was able to get through it with the help of her aunt and Zo, who along with a few of Irk's most trusted friends, made sure that their fallen leader was sent off properly. Zo gave Myah Irk's jewelry and the keys to his favorite car, his midnight blue Mercedes Benz 600. The car alone was worth over a hundred-thousand-dollars easily, but Myah knew that nothing would take away the guilt that she would feel for the rest of her life.

Zo was now in charge of Irk's multi-million-dollar drug empire, and he ran it just as he knew Irk would have. Every week, Myah would receive five-thousand-dollars in the form of a cashier's check, which she saved.

Tony couldn't attend the funeral because he was still recovering in the hospital. His nose was severely broken, and he sustained a fractured cheekbone. Henry had beaten him so badly that he had internal bleeding that had to be taken care of. Myah knew that if it wasn't for him returning when he did, she might not have been alive today.

As she turned the corner of Brown Boulevard, she thought about Nikki. Her rapist was never found. She was now seeing a therapist twice a week in order to deal with the trauma she had endured because of it. Myah knew that Nikki would never be able to trust men again. She also dropped out of school and returned back home to her parents' estate.

While Myah was in deep thought, she heard someone call her name. When she turned around, she recognized Keisha, who was wearing a pullover sweatshirt and a pair of dark blue jeans. She stopped in order for Keisha to catch up. She was coming from the park that was just up the street from where they both were now standing. Myah smiled once Keisha got closer. "Hey, girl! How's it going?" she asked in a pleasant tone of voice.

Keisha wasn't smiling. Her hands stayed inside of her sweatshirt pockets. As she stood face to face with Myah, she looked around as if she wanted to tell her a secret.

Myah thought that Keisha was acting strangely, but never paid any mind to what she was doing with her hands. As she continued to look at Keisha's face, which was still badly scarred, Keisha pulled out an envelope and said in a low voice, "I guess it was Tit 4 Tat huh?" Myah looked confused since she didn't know what Keisha was talking about. When she handed Myah the envelope, she looked inside and saw the original eight pictures that Keisha had taken of Myah and Nikki that night at her apartment, along with the negatives.

When Keisha started to walk off, Myah stopped her and asked," Why are you giving me these now?" Keisha looked up and with tearfilled eyes simply said, "It was never worth it. The price I paid because of them was never worth it." With that, she continued on down the block never once looking back.

Myah had always known that Keisha was behind the extortion scheme, but after what happened in school when those girls sliced her face up, nothing more was ever said about it. Myah placed the envelope in her pocket and continued walking thinking to herself, "What goes around, comes back around and that payback is a bitch!" At that moment, she experienced a sharp pain in the lower part of her stomach, which caused her to become nauseous. She looked around, but saw no one. She recognized the signs and knew that her suspicious were true. She was pregnant with Irk's baby, and she planned on keeping it...

...It Ain't Over! Oh No, It Ain't Over...

Four Months Later...

Deciding to call it quits after a day of shopping, Luscious and her girlfriend Desiree hopped into Desiree's boyfriend's brand new 2001 Range Rover Sport SUV to head back over to the Bronx. After spending all afternoon in Manhattan, picking up clothes that Luscious knew she would need because of her pregnancy, she was exhausted.

She was four months and her stomach was showing every bit of it. By going through two natural births with her first two kids, Luscious knew that for this one, they were going to have to give her plenty of drugs in order for her to endure the pain that she knew she was going to experience.

At four months, her stomach was already the size of a men's basketball. The doctor informed her that she was going to have twins, and that they were developing so quickly that he may have to induce labor earlier then the expected 39 weeks.

All of the clothes she had now in her closet were starting to feel too tight, thus the reason for the shopping spree. She used the money that she got after selling her boyfriend's Lincoln Navigator, since she was the one whose name was on the title and it was she that had registered it.

Two Months Earlier...

The police had informed her that the truck was left in one of the Clarkson University's parking lot and that she would have to come and pick it up or risk losing it. Knowing how much the truck was worth, Luscious acted quickly and had her friend Desiree drive her up to Potsdam, New York in order to retrieve the vehicle.

Once there, she learned that her boyfriend, the father of her unborn twins, had been killed by a young college girl that had attended the University months earlier. Even though the case was closed, the name of the young girl wasn't withheld due to the fact that she was 18 years of age, so she was of legal age to be put into the public records.

After providing the police with the proper ID in order to prove that she was the person whose name was on the title of the luxury SUV, she paid the compound fee and drove off. She was lucky that she had a good friend such as Desiree there with her, because when she found out what happened to Henry, she lost it all and had to be consoled for at least an hour before she was able to get back on the road to head home.

They had stayed in a motel along the way, since the 8 hour drive was too tiring for Luscious, especially after learning the news that she did earlier.

Desiree tried to keep her mind off of the death of Henry by keeping her occupied, but once Luscious was alone in her bed and able to think about what had happened, she became not only emotional, but extremely pissed off, that he came all this way to fuck around, when he had a perfectly good looking and willing piece of ass at home.

She got even more upset when she thought about how Henry let a girl young enough to be his daughter, trick him out of his life.

Luscious decided that night that she was going to find out who this Myah Johnson really was and possibly get even for making her unborn twins fatherless and her once again looking for a good man.

"You heard what the officer said right? She was a student at that school Clarkson University, so all we have to do is find out her last known address and I'm sure we can take care of the rest." Desire stated trying to get Luscious out of the grieving mood that she was in. Little did she know, Luscious was already two steps ahead of her. She was already plotting out her plan for revenge.

When Myah learned that her boyfriend Irk had died at the hands of Henry, she was distraught not only mentally, but physically as well. Now that her body was beginning to change, because she was pregnant, Myah had to start thinking about the future and how she as going to raise this baby alone without a father.

She remembered her mother and how she use to complain about how hard it was to raise a child without any help or a father figure. Even though Myah wasn't hurting for money or support from her family and friends, she knew that raising this child without its father, who would be able to provide the things that she knew any child would need mentally, would be a difficult task in itself.

Henry not only killed her mother, leaving her without parents to raise her, but he also killed those close to her which weighed heavily on her mind.

"If only I would of told Det. Williamson, and Irk what I was trying to do, maybe things would have turned out differently. Maybe Irk would still be alive to share in his baby's future." She thought to herself as she laid in her bed in her Bronx apartment, that she had kept because of the memories it had of Irk and their short, but special time they shared together.

For awhile, Myah blamed herself for what happened to Irk. No matter now many people tried to get her to see that she had nothing to do with his death, Myah still place the blame squarely on her shoulders.

Preparing for motherhood was starting to dominate her thoughts more and more, which to her aunt and uncle was a relief. They both watched helplessly as their niece slipped in and out of depression for about two months after coming home from Potsdam.

No matter what they said or did, nothing would bring Myah comfort. The guilt she placed on herself far out weighed anything that they could do to make her believe that she shouldn't hold herself responsible for what she couldn't prevent.

Once they learned that she was pregnant, at first, they didn't approve and were totally against it, but when they realized that Myah was slowly starting to come out of her self-imposed prison that she had placed herself in, they thought differently. Especially when they were informed that she was going to keep it.

To Myah, keeping the baby wasn't a decision she made lightly. Knowing that she was young and truly not ready for a baby was something that she had to think about. Also the fact that she didn't believe in abortion, made her decision even more difficult. But what really pushed her to keep the baby was the fact that it was Irk's and knowing, that a part of him was growing inside of her was the deciding factor as to why she kept the baby. If she couldn't have Irk with her, she knew that having his child was as close she would be to keeping his memory alive.

Now that she was 4 moths into her pregnancy, her body and mind was slowly preparing her for motherhood. Knowing that her aunt never had kids, Myah couldn't ask the questions that she wanted to without upsetting her.

Since Mary was unable to have kids herself, because of complications, with her uterus, she always felt awkward whenever the subject of child birth came up. Myah knew that it hurt her aunt deeply, and part of the reason why Mary loved Myah so much was because Myah gave her the opportunity to be the mother that she always wanted to be.

When Myah let Zo know that she was pregnant with Irk's baby, he become her biggest supporter. He made sure that Myah needed for nothing. Some would have thought that it was his baby that Myah was carrying by the way he fussed over her.

Myah knew that Zo would make a good Godfather for her child, since he already thought of it as his own. He wanted to be a part of the baby's life even before he/ she was even born. Knowing that her child would be very well taken care of made her decision that much easier.

The day, that Zo woke up from surgery, and learned that his best friend had died from a single gunshot wound to the chest, and the guilt of knowing that he couldn't protect him had set in, he couldn't sleep, eat or see anyone for a week straight.

Zo blamed himself for Irk death, since it was his hands that Irk had trusted his life in. Every time he closed his eyes, he could see everything that happened that day as if it was yesterday.

He remembered telling Irk after hearing the three quick shots that Henry had let off as they were getting inside of his car. "Get Down! Get Down!" at that exact moment, Zo felt two shots rip through his back, which caused him to fall instantly. Before he blacked out from the pain, he looked up only to see Irk slumped in the passenger seat with his eyes opened and a giant bloody hole in the center of his chest. He pulled out his cell and pressed 9-1-1, calling for help.

The next thing he knew, he was in a hospital bed unable to move because of the pain of being shot and the emergency surgery he had, to remove the scraps of the hollow point tips that were lodged in the lower part of his back.

Zo knew that he was lucky to be alive, but knowing that his friend of many years wasn't would haunt and torment him for the rest of his life,

For the first few weeks after Irk's funeral, the transition of taking over Irk's roll was not so smooth. Even though Zo was groomed for the position knowing, that one day he may be called upon to do so in the event, that something happened to Irk, not everyone was on board like he thought they would be.

There were some that tried their hand and tested Zo's authority and those that did quickly found out that he was just as ruthless, if not more, than Irk was. By doing this, he not only stop those that tried him, he also sent the message that he wasn't the one to be played with. He was in charge whether they liked it or not.

He kept a tight circle of trusted people around him

just like Irk did. He made Taz his lieutenant and went about the business of running the empire that Irk had established years ago.

The responsibilities that was bestowed upon Zo was nothing since it was he that really ran the daily operation for Irk anyway. But now that Irk was gone, Zo was now responsible for feeding those under him. Everybody had to eat and it was known throughout the city that if you worked for Irk, you ate very well.

After learning just how much Irk's empire was truly worth, Zo was amazed. Not only did he not know that Irk was worth millions, thanks to his bank statements that were left in Irk's Soundview apartment, which Zo was now living in, but that he had a major connection with the Dominicans that with or without Irk's help, were going to move their product throughout the city.

Once they knew that it was Zo that was now in charge, they gave him the same deal that they gave Irk. Zo was more than happy to continue the relationship with them, since he knew that the coke he was getting was far better than any he had seen on the streets.

Now after four months of being in charge, running the day to day operation, Zo was ready to relax a little. Not a day went by that he didn't think of his homie Irk. He knew that he would never see his friend again and that all he would have of him was the memories that they shared. But when Zo found out that Myah was pregnant, and the baby was Irk's, Zo knew that Irk would have wanted him to spoil the child. He made sure that Myah and her unborn child would need for nothing as long as he was around. This gave Zo the opportunity to give back to the one person that helped him to be who he was today. He also knew that since he wasn't able to protect his friend while he was alive, he wasn't going to let anything happen to his child.

Knowing that everyone who wanted to pay their respects to Irk before he was laid to rest, couldn't attend his funeral, since it was only set up for close friends and family, Zo decided to hold a memorial concert that would allow all of those that couldn't attend the funeral the opportunity to pay their respect and to celebrate his life through music.

Since money was no object, considering over the last four months, Zo and his crew made a profit far beyond what they had expected, Zo wasn't going to slack on anything.

The concert was going to be free for all those that could get into the Nassau Coliseum before the doors could close due to overcrowding.

Those that were fortunate enough to get in would be treated to 3 hours of musical celebration that would range from Rap to R&B with such names as Keith Sweat, Total, DMX, Jay Z, Mobb Deep, KRS-One, Peter Gunz and Tyriq, Eve, the Lox, and 112 just to name a few. Zo had solid confirmation from others that were definitely going to perform a special Tribute to a fallen soldier that was very well respected.

Zo had his legal team obtain the proper permits, contracts, and paperwork that were needed to lock down the Coliseum for that one day. He also made sure that the money he would need in order to ensure that every person that attended would have a good time was there along with the security firm that he was going to use to protect not only the concert goers, but the artists that were to perform as well.

Once he had the go ahead and the date set; Zo had

his street team circulate fliers to let the population know. Everything was done on the first come basis and once the allowed capacity was reached, security was told to close all doors, no exceptions.

Zo knew that once the word got out, everyone and their mother would be begging to get a hold of a ticket. Out of the 25,000 tickets to be given out, Zo and his crew held 1,000 of them in order to be distributed among friends and family. He made certain that Myah and those close to her had their V.I.P tickets that included backstage access to meet the artists, as well as access to go anywhere she would want to go.

All in all, the total cost of it all was close to three hundred thousand dollars and that wasn't even including what he would pay for the catering service that he was planning to hire to cater the event.

When Zo called Myah after learning that everything was a go, she was so surprised by it all that she literally cried the entire conversation that they had.

Myah knew that Irk would never be forgotten, and Zo made sure of that. She was not surprised by how he had stepped up in Irk's absence. What did surprise her was the fact that they got along the way they did. For a long time, Myah had thought that Zo didn't like her being with Irk, but as time passed, and her and Irk's relationship began to get more serious, Zo started to warn up to the idea that she was going to be around. Now, after Irk's death, their relationship as friends had gotten a lot better. They became as close as friends could get.

The day before the concert, Zo had one of his workers go and take Myah shopping in order to buy an outfit for the big event. He knew that since she was pregnant she would feel a little apprehensive about being around a lot of people being how big she was and knowing that she didn't have the figure that she used to have, that would make men's heads turn whenever she walked into a place.

Even though Myah didn't think she was still beautiful, Zo thought differently. In his eyes, she was still one of the baddest girls he's seen, pregnant and all, and he wasn't alone. Everyone in his immediate circle of friend also thought that Myah was a dime piece, but none of them would ever let it be known, knowing how Zo viewed her and who she represented.

After spending a couples of hours at the mall of her choice, Dre escorted Myah to New Visions, a hair and nail salon in the Bronx, and told her, "Zo thought you may want to get your hair and nails done before he had you and your friends picked up for the concert. If there is anything else you need, just let me know." Myah couldn't believe how much Zo was going out of his way in order to make her feel special. "Nah Dre, this is good. I do appreciate all that you have done today. I know I was a pain in the ass at the mall, but I just didn't think anything looked good on me. It's not like I still have the body that I use to have and I hate wearing these baggy ass clothes. But today, you and Zo made me feel like my old self again."

"Don't thank me, thank Zo. I'm just here to make sure you get what you need." Dre said trying to hide the true feelings he had for Myah, but knowing who she was kept him from making a move. The whole time he was with her, he has done nothing but fantasize about her. Her ass was still one of the phattest he'd seen and now that she was pregnant, her tits were a whole cup size larger, which made them look bigger than they normally were. Dre would steal glances every chance he got, knowing that she didn't have a clue as to what he was truly thinking.

Little did he know, Myah did notice the glances he was taking. She didn't mind though. In fact, it made her feel good knowing that she still had it.

Once she was finished at the salon, she gave Dre a call to let him know that she was ready to leave. Before he arrived, Myah called Nikki to let her know that she would be back in Long Island in about an hour or so, and that she was going to have Dre drop her off at her house.

Nikki and Myah's friendship grew even stronger after learning the drama that they both had been through. For a while, Nikki had completely shut herself off from the world. Not even Myah could get through to her. It was only after Myah told her about the pregnancy that Nikki started to come around, interacting with her friends and family again.

Now after a few months of therapy and having their family as their support system, both girls were almost completely recovered. Nothing would erase the drama that both of them went through, but as they say. "Time will heal all wounds, mental or physical."

Myah tried to get Nikki to come to the concert with her, hoping that she would say yes this time around, but as always, Nikki declined the offer without giving reasons why. Myah already knew the reason why. Nikki was still not ready to be around men or large crowds. After learning that she'd been raped, that ordeal in itself was mentally playing with her mind. Nikki felt vulnerable and no matter how much her parents paid a therapist, Nikki knew that no one would truly understand what she'd been through or how scared she was to let another man touch her, including her own father. Myah understood, but she tried her hand anyway, hoping that Nikki would surprise her and say yes.

So once again, Myah knew she'd be forced to either go alone or invite some of her girlfriends along for a night of celebrating, celebrating the life of her late boyfriend Dirk "Irk" Wright.

Day of the Concert...

Desiree had invited Luscious, her cousin Tyesha, and her friend Briana to go with her to Long Island for the concert. They were all about to pile into Luscious's Lincoln Navigator. The truck had more than enough room to accommodate all four girls and then some.

As soon as Desiree opened the backdoor, the running board of the truck automatically slid out in order for her to step up into it. Once she sat down in the light grey leather seat it instantly made her feel like she was in a club's V.I.P section, which she's been in plenty of over the years.

Brianna was elected the designated driver, since Luscious had a hard time getting behind the wheel now that she was pregnant. Tyesha, who was Desiree's first cousin, sat up front while Brianna climbed into the driver seat.

Both girls were drop dead gorgeous and knew it. When Desiree asked her cousin if she wanted to go to the concert, that her boyfriend was doing security for, Tyesha didn't have to think twice about it.

At first, Luscious was a little hesitate about being around so many people in her condition, but after Desiree, Briana, and Tyesha convinced her that going out will make her feel better, she was all for it.

Once they saw the exit for Hempstead, Brianna made her way off the ramp and continued to drive down Hempstead Avenue towards the Nassau Coliseum's parking lot. There were so many people walking around making their way toward the many entrances that were located around the building.

After finding a spot to park the truck, all four girls exited the vehicle and were instantly overwhelmed by just how many people were trying to get in. Luckily, Desiree's boyfriend, who was standing near the entrance, saw them and waved them over.

"Damn! It took ya'll long enough. I was beginning to think that ya'll weren't gonna make it." Marquez stated with a slight attitude. Desiree always had a thing for the thugged out type and Marquez was her thug.

"We left early, but the traffic getting here was crazy." Desiree replied as she walked up to him to give him a kiss. After getting his feel on, Marquez opened the door to let them inside and had one of his guards escort all four of them to their seats.

The seats that he had gotten for them were so close to the stage that they would practically be a part of the show. As they made their way to their seats, all eyes were on them as people tried to see if they were somebody they should know.

While Luscious and her friends found their seats, Myah and her friends were just arriving in their super stretched champagne color Cadillac Escalade limo. When it stopped in front of the main entrance, two security guards walked up to the back door and escorted Myah and her crew inside to their seats. They were seated to the right of the main stage, where they were surrounded by celebrities both in the music and show business. They were all there to celebrate the life of a man that had influenced so many during his lifetime.

As the last person made their way through the door, security was told to secure the entrances and not to let another person in. Before the opening performance was to take the stage, the MC for the night came out from behind the black curtain to welcome everyone and to announce each act.

"Heyyy, how is everybody doing?" The crowd cheered their answer "Fineeeee!"

"Alright then. Before we get this show started, let's give a round of applause to the man that was able to bring this all together. Zo! Where are you big fella?" Everyone looked around as if they were trying to find him as well. Zo raised up from his chair which was located right next to his Lt. Taz. Zo was surrounded by his entourage of security and his top Lieutenants that ran his empire from the top down. Everyone applauded once they saw him standing. "There you go! Let me say thank you. Thank you for giving all of us the opportunity to celebrate Irk's life." Everyone was still on their feet cheering as Zo waved his hand around.

After about a minute, the MC came back to the mic and then said a few words about Irk and before he ended, in order for the first act to open up, the last thing he did before leaving the stage was to recognize Irk's number one lady. "And before we get started, let's also give a round of applause to Irk's better half." Everyone started to laugh at the MC's attempt at a joke. "Myah Johnson!"

As soon as Myah's name was announced by the MC, Luscious and Desiree stopped what they were doing and looked up towards the stage. They were now able to put a face to the name of the person that Luscious knew was responsible for Henry's death...

Coming Soon!

Tit 4 Tat 3
(It Ain't Over!)

About The Author

A.L. Strange is a graduate of Potsdam College. He has a B.A. in Political Science and an Associates in Sociology. He is from New York and is currently residing in FCI Loretto.

Strange is co-author of the book "Beyond Repair" with Frasier Boy and the author of "Beguiled" that will be out soon.

NEW VISION
PUBLICATION
PRESENTS
Damaged
—A gritty and raw urban thriller which grabs you from the very first page and won't let you go until the very end...
PARENTAL ADVISORY EXPLICIT CONTENT
A NOVEL BY
LSD GONZALES

Damaged

"Ladies and gentlemen of the jury, I ask you to please do not let the defendant's baby face fool you. Yes, her story of abuse is heartfelt, but we are not here for that. This is not an abuse case-this is a manslaughter case. These are nothing but allegations. There is nothing on record to support her claims. However, the evidence shows that the defendant is a ruthless, vicious killer and deserves to be prosecuted to the fullest extent. The victims in this case deserve justice, and only you, ladies and gentlemen of this jury, can provide that justice."

How the fuck can justice be served when there's not one black or Hispanic on the fucking jury? I can't believe this shit! I thought to myself as the prosecutor kept running his fucking mouth.

"Ladies and gentlemen of the jury, take a look at the defendant. Her baby face still holds a sense of innocence, but her heart speaks murder. As a father, a brother and a servant of this community, I can no longer tolerate our youth running around this city acting if they were grown up. When do we, law-abiding citizens, put a stop to the madness that our youths are engaging in today? In my twenty years of service, I have never witnessed a case of such malice. Since when do kids go around murdering their parents simply because they don't want to follow the rules their parents put in place? Today, ladies and gentlemen of the jury, you have the opportunity to send all out of control youth in this city a clear message, that we, the people, will not tolerate any disrespect towards our parents. I'm asking you on behalf of the people of Philadelphia to do the right thing, and find the defendant guilty as charged."

It took the jury less then three hours to determine my fate. I glanced over at my lawyer. He appeared confident, as he had since the trial began.

The judge looked at me with a perverted smile. "Will the defendant please rise!" The judge addressed the jury foreman. "Has the jury reach a verdict?"

I smiled and began screaming at the jury. "You white muthafuckas can't wait to send me away! Fuck you all! I don't give a fuck! I rather be in jail than in this courtroom where you racist assholes wanna sit up there pretending like you know what happened. Fuck you! Fuck you!"

The spectators in the courtroom went bananas.

"Quiet! Quiet! Quiet in the courtroom!" the judge shouted, ordering the deputies to cuff me up immediately. "Young lady, one more outburst like that, and I swear I will charge you with--"

"Kiss my Puerto Rican ass, you white devil!"

"Jury foreman, please read the verdict," the judge ordered.

"Your Honor, we the jury find the defendant--"

"I don't give a fuck what you white muthafuckas think of me!" This shit was like a bad dream. I looked at the jury and shook my head in amazement. Twelve members of my community decided my fate, and not one had the courage to look at me... not one!

"Young lady--"

"Fuck you, Your Honor!"

"Can the foreman please read the verdict now!"

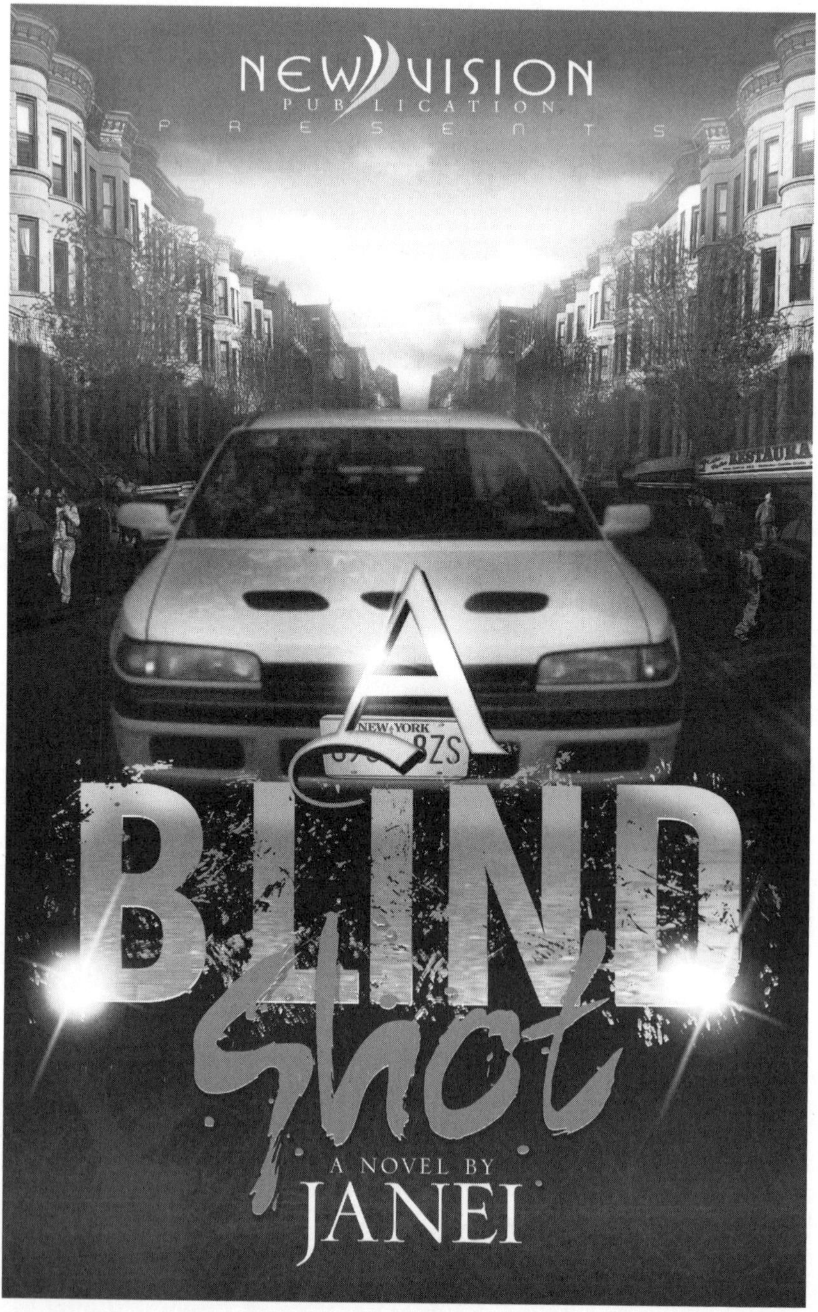
NEW VISION
PUBLICATION
PRESENTS
A
BLIND
Shot
A NOVEL BY
JANEI

Chapter One

The car moved slowly through the streets of Harlem, in New York City. Its two occupants were watching as merchants closed their stores for the night. The sun had set an hour ago, but the sidewalk remained crowded with people. They surveyed block after block like tourists fascinated by the sights and sounds of an urban legend. Trey and Butter were far from that. Nor were they new-comers in this part of town. Both of them were born in Harlem Hospital and raised in the surrounding neighborhoods, from Central Park North up into the Polo Grounds. They knew their way around these streets like the backs of their hands.

A few girls standing around glanced at their ten year old Mazda and quickly dismissed the both of them as nobodies. In truth, these two had quite a reputation, though an anonymous one. They were the stick-up men that had robbed at least a dozen grocery stores, drug spots, and jewelry-wearing cash-heavy ballers in the last month alone.

Trey had the radio blasting hardcore gangsta rap, as he played with the barrel of a Magnum he held out of sight of onlookers. Butter maneuvered the Mazda down several side streets and came to a stop at a red light. On the corner, several young Black men were laughing and joking at a card table. A small radio near them atop a milk crate was playing oldies. The loud music from the Mazda caught their attention as it idled at the light. Trey stared hard at them, and eventually he was noticed and the men stared back.

Finally, one of them yelled to him, "What the fuck you looking at, man?"

As the light changed, Trey pointed the Magnum at the men, and they all dove to the ground for cover. With one shot, he blasted their tiny radio to bits. The roar of the Magnum echoed on the street. As the men continued to hug the ground, Trey could be heard laughing over the sound of the car's music as the Mazda sped away.

Trey, at twenty-two years old, had spent half of his life in and out of jail. He was never without a gun. He got his first taste of its power when he got his hands on the .357 Magnum while in junior high school. One day, he watched as a local heroin dealer named Dax ran from cops, and tossed the gun under an old dirty mattress. After the police caught Dax five blocks away, beat him and hauled him off to jail, Trey retrieved the weapon. The first thing he noticed was how heavy it was, but it was beautiful and he instantly fell in love with it. He carried it all the time, even to school, and waited for the opportunity to use it.

One day, there were some school bullies picking on some weaker kids. Then, they approached Trey. They told him he was going to have to start paying punk dues if he wanted to continue to come to school. Though Trey was never fond of school in the first place, he saw this as what he had been waiting for. He pulled out the Magnum, and before any of them could react, he smashed the biggest one across the face with the heavy weapon. As the kid lay on the ground holding his shattered jaw, Trey stripped him and his friends of money, jewelry and every stitch of clothing, then sent them running home bare ass naked.

He was arrested the next day, and although they never got the Magnum, he was charged and convicted of assault and robbery. At thirteen, he began his journey in and out of juvenile detention and prison.

Butter, on the other hand, fared well growing up. Though older than Trey at twenty-seven, he had never been arrested, even though he had been pulling robberies for years. Butter was always a thinker and a planner, and was often willing to pull a job if it could be done with the least amount of violence.

He had met Trey two years ago when he worked for a job center in the Harlem State Office Building. Trey was on parole at the time and was required to get a job. He began visiting the center just to keep his parole officer off his back. Butter, who did filing and record keeping, talked to Trey every time he came by, and the two started hanging out. Before long, Butter began to join Trey on the armed robberies he boasted so much about.

Butter grew to not only appreciate the money they made, but the thrill and cunningness of robbing so many people and never getting caught. It became a game to him. Yet, Trey's explosive and sometimes violent temper spoiled that fun, and more than once he put them both at risk of getting killed.

Now, as they cruised down the streets of Harlem to the next job, he willed everything to go as planned.

After several more turns, Butter finally parked the car across the street from an old tenement. He reached over and turned off the radio.

"What'd you do that for?" Trey asked.

"Yo, what the fuck is wrong with you?"

Trey gave him a curious look, phony as it was. "What are you talkin' 'bout?"

"Don't play dumb with me, Trey!" Butter said. "That was real stupid back there."

Trey smiled and held up the Magnum. "Did you see them run? Them niggas was scared shitless."

Butter shook his head. "It's not funny. That's the type

of shit that'll get us knocked."

"Just chill, Butter," said Trey. "Why you get so riled up all the time?"

Butter said nothing else. He continued to watch the building across the street as he loaded his twelve gauge shotgun. He had never fired the big weapon, using it mostly for intimidation. However, he knew that if the time came to smoke someone with it, they would be splattered. He checked his watch. "They should be coming out in a few, get ready."

"I'm ready, homie," Trey said, holding up the Magnum.

"Where's the masks?"

"I thought you brought them."

Butter turned toward him. "What do you mean you thought I brought them? I told you to pack the damn masks before we left."

"Well, I forgot. I thought you was gonna get them. Fuck the masks!"

"What do you mean, fuck the masks?" screamed Butter. "The point is not to be seen!"

"No, the point is to get paid! So we make do without them," replied Trey just as loudly.

Butter shook his head at the incompetence that Trey could show at times. Suddenly, the doors of the tenement opened and three young men came out and stood in front of the building. One of them carried a large black garbage bag.

"Show time!" said Trey, and Butter gunned the engine...

NEW VISION
PUBLICATION

P.O. Box 2815
Stockbridge, GA 30281

Or

P.O. Box 310367
Jamaica, NY 11431

Order Form

Name: _____

Address: _____

City: _____ **State:** _____ **Zip:** _____

Qty	Title	Price	Total
	Tit 4 Tat Part 1	$15.00	
	A Blind Shot	$15.00	
	Damaged	$15.00	
	Tit 4 Tat Part 2	$15.00	
	-Coming Soon-		
	Thicker Than Blood	$15.00	
	Shank	$15.00	
		Subtotal	
	...Shipping Charges...	**Shipping**	_____
	Media Mail First Book .... $3.85 Each additional book..............$1.50	**Total**	$_____

(No Personal Checks Accepted)
Make Institutional Checks or Money Orders payable to:
New Vision Publication

NEW VISION
PUBLICATION

P.O. Box 2815
Stockbridge, GA 30281

Or

P.O. Box 310367
Jamaica, NY 11431

Order Form

Name: _____

Address: _____

City: _____ **State:** _____ **Zip:** _____

Qty	Title	Price	Total
	Tit 4 Tat Part 1	$15.00	
	A Blind Shot	$15.00	
	Damaged	$15.00	
	Tit 4 Tat Part 2	$15.00	
	-Coming Soon-		
	Thicker Than Blood	$15.00	
	Shank	$15.00	
		Subtotal	
	...Shipping Charges...	**Shipping**	_____
	Media Mail First Book ……..... $3.85 Each additional book…………..$1.50	**Total**	$_____

(No Personal Checks Accepted)
Make Institutional Checks or Money Orders payable to:
New Vision Publication